*To all the writers, bloggers, and reviewers who have support-*
*ed me on the hike that is writing.*
*You've made it all the less steep.*

# RUINS

## OF

# SMOKE

## A SMOKESMITHS TALE
### Prequel Novella

JOÃO F. SILVA

First paperback edition August 2023

*Edited by Sarah Chorn*

*Proofread by Ed Crocker*

*Cover Design by MIBLART*

*Interior Illustrations by CyberOni Arts*

ISBN 9781739365615 (paperback)

Published by João F. Silva

www.joaofsilva.net

# CONTENTS

# USHAR, CAPITA

## WESTERN RIFT

PA
OF BRI

# OF THE EMPIRE

ZEIRAM
BASTION

CE
IANCE

EASTERN
RIFT

YAB

*Spitfire*

*Lantern Horn*

# ONE

# THE BUILDERS

## JEHA

Silence reigned inside the Zeiram Bastion while screams filled the air outside.

Sister Jeha of the Red Sun Army held the hands of her sisters. They stood in a circle, facing each other. With eyes closed and a deep breath, she opened herself and dove into her Inner Flight.

The Essence coursed through her like a raging river, feeding clarity to her mind's eye. Jeha wasn't really sure *what* the Essence was. Maybe a deity or, perhaps, the course of nature itself? But she didn't *need* to know—those were matters for scholars and monks—when the Essence gave life to the city in an all-connected web of invisible strings of power.

Jeha was no beginner, but to this day, there was still no feeling like opening the floodgates of enhanced awareness. It was even better than being greeted by the warm embrace of an old friend as the Essence's invisible and invigorating lines connected her to her sisters and the chaos outside the tower.

Jeha opened her eyes and let go of her battle sisters' hands. Just like her, they wore red brigandines over a white gambeson emblazoned with the emblem of the Red Sun Army. The Inner Flight was an ancient gift from the Essence to all the Army's sentinels. It tuned them all in the same key, like music instruments playing in a concert.

"We all saw it. We all *felt* it." Sister Amel stood about ten feet in front of Jeha, the deep-set wrinkles spelling out the length of her duty as a battle sister. She'd been diving into her Inner Flight since long before Jeha was born. A legend in her own right, Jeha was now her proud battle sister, sharing a bond that only death could break. "The Zeiram Bastion... No, Ushar itself is under attack. There's an open rift."

Jeha knew it to be true. The Essence allowed her to feel a foulness and, with pulses of energy and little harmless sparks in her mind, begged Jeha to destroy it. "Let us go, sisters. The Essence calls, so let's not make her wait. We must protect the Red Sun King!"

"Lead us, Sister Jeha. To victory or death."

"To victory or death!" the sisters roared.

Jeha didn't need the battle sisters to tell her how much she meant to them. With the Essence, she could *feel* it. Theirs was a kinship that went beyond words and deeds.

A true bond that had only strengthened over the years. She could sense the pride in their hearts and the immense gratitude washing over them. They were chosen. Just like Jeha, her battle sisters had been at death's door, and the Essence had given them another chance to do something more. Jeha's heart stirred at the memory. She had accepted death as a way out, but the Essence had called and bonded her to the sentinels. The blissful warmth of sisterly love and friendship was a shock at first, but it soon became a reason to live. A reason to be grateful she had chosen to live.

"The Red Sun King is counting on us, as is every man and woman in Ushar. The capital must not fall. We're the King's sentinels. We *won't* let it fall," Jeha roared.

"To victory or death!"

More than the Essence or the Red Sun King, Jeha and her sisters would fight for one another, as they always had.

She led the way and opened the door to the terrace. Her heart filled with fire at the sight. Thunder boomed in the dark of night as the sky was illuminated by firelight. Parts of the city walls were burning and explosions sounded from every direction. The skies were peppered with flying creatures. A horrible stench seared her nostrils. If wrongness had a smell, it would be this. The Deceiver must be back. His shadowlings were pouring into the Empire's capital. Something was different this time, though. There was more urgency in the Essence's call.

"Can you feel it?" she asked. "The Deceiver must have found an avatar."

Sister Amel placed her gauntlet on Jeha's pauldron. "I can, Sister. Let us fulfil our duty."

Jeha nodded, and the passion and pride borrowed from Sister Amel turned into resolve. She needed a weapon, so she tapped into the Essence's infinite power.

*Please.*

She felt the battle sisters beg for the same.

Smoke threads appeared out of the air, contorting and shaping themselves into weapons. Threads of smoke floated out of Jeha's dark smoke spear, blending with the air, even though her grasp was tight as though it was made of wood and steel. As always, the smoke spear was light and deadlier than any other weapon she could wield. One by one, her sisters conjured their weapons—long pikes, spears, axes, and battle hammers of smoke.

Jeha walked over to the Bastion's battlement, looked out of the crenel, and took a deep breath. A wave of warmth flooded her. Strength from her battle sisters. There was no room for fear or hesitation before a battle. Once again, her gaze found Sister Amel, whose weary eyes did not dare break away from hers.

Jeha climbed the parapet, looked down from the cliff upon which the Bastion had been built, and jumped. "For the Red Sun!"

She did not look up as she dropped. Her sisters would jump right after her.

The powerful flow of the Essence spread across the capital city, permeating bodies and buildings alike. It was invisible to most, but Jeha was a sentinel, chosen by the deity to protect its slow spread across Ushar. She clung onto the Essence with everything she had. Bathed in it; became one with it. Her plunge halted well before she reached the ground, and her body started floating, then flying upwards.

*Faith is power. Thank you.*

Without believing the all-seeing, all-knowing Essence, there would be nothing to take. Faith had to come first.

The Essence's invisible web held Jeha and the battle sisters in the sky, and carried them at incredible speeds. She didn't need to look out for her battle sisters. She could *feel* them flying in formation behind her, like a flock of falcons tearing through the sky.

The cold wind bit Jeha's face, as though she had disturbed its natural course. The sky was filled with demonic creatures, and Ushar's streets were littered with monsters just as horrendous. A constant buzz rang in her ears, often interrupted by lightning bolts hitting the ground.

The beautiful city of Ushar, pride of the Builders, was burning.

Her people had designed the city in harmony with the Essence. Canals distributed water from the Southern

Ocean across the city. Trees lined every road and avenue. Ivy covered the brickwork and moss adorned rooftops. All that was the way for the Essence to thrive, giving its invisible lines natural markers to settle on. Without nature peppering the capital, the Essence would slowly decay, and with her demise, Ushar would perish. Destroying this perfectly designed architecture would leave the city devoid of the Essence's blessing forever.

Jeha watched with horror as a building-sized beast spat fire, burning a Red Sun temple. Its huge tusks and spiked, scaly skin warped its humanoid shape into something hideous. The demons were stronger than they should be. Bolder than she'd remembered. In that moment, her confidence wavered. She'd faced the Deceiver's shadowlings before, but never had they done such damage. Never had they *dared*.

Her skin prickled, and she swallowed, promptly flooded by a wave of strength from her battle sisters.

A baleful shriek turned louder, and something hit her pauldron. When Jeha turned to look, a bat-like monstrosity latched onto her armour with its claws. She fumbled and buckled under the weight of the creature but held herself together without falling. The creature's maw bit into her armour, its talons piercing her skin. A foul stench oozed from the beast, blurring her sight. The fiend was a whole nine feet of scales, membranous wings, and long, thin limbs.

A rush of strength and resolve permeated Jeha. *Focus!* She tried to shove the creature away while other beasts attacked her battle sisters. She swung her spear arm through the air and stabbed the shadowling with all her might. The creature squealed as dark, viscous fluid poured from the wound.

Jeha followed through, thrusting the weapon even deeper and pulling it out, separating herself from the fiend. Her gauntlet caught a blow from the shadowling's right arm and, with gritted teeth, she held the beast for another stab of her smoke spear. The weapon cut effortlessly through the air and bit the creature in the neck. Despite the howls of pain, it still lived.

Jeha readied herself, spear pointing forwards. She called to the Essence and the smoke spear grew, becoming twice its original length. Jeha swung and cut the creature's neck, separating its head from the body. With no time to rest, she rushed to aid her battle sisters. The shadowlings shouldn't be this strong. They'd always been smaller and weaker than a plate-armoured soldier, just in bigger numbers. Panic grew in the depths of her heart as fear crept in. The garrisons could never have prepared for such an attack. Why would they? There had been no reason to believe the enemy would come with both numbers and might. *Can the shadowlings be pushed away this time?*

Sister Amel was fighting three of the bat-like shadowlings, darting from left to right, back and forth. The sky held no secrets for Amel as she evaded their brutal blows with polished movements.

Jeha struck one of the fiends with her spear. The creature yelped, but large talons shot back at her and cut her cheek, the wound burning intensely. Jeha gritted her teeth and stabbed the creature, watching for the other scourge. They'd never been able to cut her like that. A chill went through her, but she could hardly afford emotions when so many lives depended on her. If the battle sisters faltered, Ushar would fall, the empire would collapse, and millions would crumble to the Deceiver.

"Sister Amel, stay with the first five squads and contain the threat. I'll take the other five and make for the royal chambers," Jeha roared.

Sister Amel glanced at her. "What about closing the rift?"

"We'll have to trust that the Smoke Riders will see it through. Our priority is protecting the Red Sun King."

Sister Amel swallowed and nodded. She turned to face the beasts, and Jeha felt the woman calling the battle sisters of the five squads to gather around her. Each bastion had a few dozen squads—surely all of them were busy with their own fiends to slay. She had no doubt they were all as occupied as she was. When the Deceiver struck, everyone had to fight.

*With me!* Jeha called the sisters under her command, temporarily forfeiting the bond with all the other sentinels. It was more trust than obedience. Five squads of battle sisters listened and fell behind her, flying through the night towards the Palace of Brilliance. Jeha wished in her heart for the Red Sun King to be safe. He was the Essence's avatar. Without him, humanity would buckle against the Deceiver and the Essence's flow would cease.

For now, Jeha relied on the Essence, picking up speed as she shot through the air and avoided the beasts on her tail. The deity gave her the ability to fly after her first successful Inner Flight, but it had also granted her strength, power, and speed, and gave her an awareness of herself and all those touched by it, as though she had intrinsic knowledge of how her body moved; how strong it was. She could almost see things half a second before they happened.

She shivered at the sight of the chaos beneath her as she flew. Citizens ran for cover and beasts burst through doors and windows, mindless slaughter abundant. Her stomach turned. They fought their way through the sky and towards the royal chambers amid the foul odour of the Deceiver's beasts. If she was right and he had indeed found an avatar, he wouldn't be far.

Tapping into the Essence again, the Red Sun King was a large pool of warm light channelling the Essence throughout the city, acting as her anchor. He was safe, though it was hard to know for how long. She could also feel the Deceiver's rift from across the city, pulsing with energy, connecting this world to another, bringing more shadowlings in.

"The city reeks of foulness." Sister Rosach's words were pregnant with fear.

Jeha nodded and flooded the sister with warmth and the fire of battle.

*One for all, Sister.*

*And all for the Red Sun.* The reply came through her mind's eye.

Countless soldiers below had fallen to the beasts, their bodies covering the bloodied cobbles. She didn't recognise any of the species of demons. They were all taller and heavier than the last the Deceiver had sent. Some spat fire while others were strong enough to demolish a castle wall. Jeha suspected something—or someone—was feeding them power the same way she and the sentinels drank from the Essence, but in a twisted manner.

Below, a group of five smokesmiths of the Red Sun Army stood their ground against a horde of hound-like beasts. The creatures' tulip-shaped heads had terrifying mouths in place of faces, lined with rows of gnashing teeth. The smokesmiths should be powerful, each with their own abilities for war and weapons similar to Jeha's. They were renowned across the world.

But they were struggling.

Their armoured gambesons were too thin to protect them. Even the abilities granted by the smoke wasn't enough to reduce the horde's numbers. They fended off the beasts by hurling smoke at them or enhancing their physical aptitudes, but it didn't make a difference.

Jeha watched a smokesmith gather a hurricane of smoke and ash before him and throw it at the incoming horde. It swirled in the air, and half of the creatures were caught in it, poisoned by the smoke. The demons that survived charged after, racing towards the weary smokesmiths.

Jeha's skin crawled and she bit her lip. Perhaps the Smoke Riders could help.

"I can't believe my eyes," said Sister Olon. "We must do something, Sister."

"I want to help. We all do. But we must make it to the Red Sun King first. Without him, we're doomed."

Sister Olon needed no further words, and they all cut through the sky above the mossy rooftops, dodging fires and avoiding the flying fiends.

Jeha landed in the courtyard of the Palace of Brilliance. The inner walls that separated the King's residence from the rest of the city had already been breached. The steel gates were bent like wet clay, the ancient brickwork had turned to ash and dust, and the battlements were still burning. Sister Shakil stopped in front of her, and they raced together towards the royal chambers with the squads on their tails.

The courtyard was littered with stones and debris, and the beautiful gardens were no more. The foul stench intensified as though they were racing towards its origin. The implications made her skin prickle. Could everyone be... dead? Without warning, lights flickered from the other side of a pavilion as a nine-foot-tall creature appeared and set its gaze on the sisters. It was fishlike but muscular, with a horn growing from its forehead that emitted flashes of light.

A Lantern Horn.

The battle sisters rushed to fight it, but the Deceiver's favourite kind of fiend was smart. Soldiers who had survived their previous attacks said the monsters seemed to know warfare tactics.

Jeha didn't plan on finding out if that was true and stabbed it. The Lantern Horn was slithery and hard to strike. The Red Sun King's shamans had tried to study Lantern Horns and learn from their powers, but their findings were limited to observations of corpses and tales from soldiers who'd survived encounters.

The Lantern Horn set its gaze on Sister Renid and caught her by surprise with a heavy blow to her chest, denting her gambeson and sending her rolling away.

"Squads Five and Six, protect our sister. Seven, Eight, and Nine, with me."

Each squad had twenty fully trained battle sisters, which gave her some comfort. Jeha sprung up, flying high enough to distance herself from the Lantern Horn. She wished for her smoke spear to lengthen, and it grew. The power of the Essence seeped through her palms as she stabbed at the Lantern Horn.

With the Essence enveloping her, there was nothing Jeha couldn't do. Her strikes were fast, each stab precise. Her smoke spear bit into the Lantern Horn and she pressed on the blade, pushing the creature down just long enough for her sisters to come to her aid and stab the monster.

She would not buckle. She would not yield.

Even severely weakened, the Lantern Horn snarled and flailed its powerful arms, looking for a target. It punched the ground and sent ripples of power in all directions, forcing Jeha and her sisters back. Stronger than she'd thought. Jeha drew her arms back and darted towards the maimed Lantern Horn, swinging. Her smoke spear crashed into the head with such power, it split the creature's skull in half, causing light to fade from its horn. Jeha was left covered in its orange blood.

She coughed blood and felt the panic of Sister Olon and the others before noticing a crimson stain in her gambeson, the metal plates torn around her stomach. The Lantern Horn had managed a blow after all.

Jeha collapsed to her knees with shock. The Essence *was* good and always provided for the worthy ones, but it couldn't perform miracles. Sentinels, smokesmiths, and anyone else gifted by the Essence healed faster than usual, but she still needed to bide her time and be careful not to make the wound worse.

She bit her lip. Time was something she didn't have.

"Sister!" Olon's voice carried the weight of concern.

"I'm fine, Sister. I will not die from this wound. Let us continue."

It was true. The wound had already started to heal. No cause for panic.

*I'm fine. Really.*

If the warmth and support from her sisters could heal, it would have. It was always like the first spark of fire on a freezing eve. It never failed to ignite her fighting spirit. They were worried for her but understood her resolve. Respected it. Cherished it.

She glanced at the royal chambers, and little pinches and pulses from the Essence drew in her mind's eye a picture of what it looked like inside. Only some walls left. The Red Sun King wasn't far. His bright presence burned like a guiding light through the Essence's invisible web. She inspected her wound again.

*Flying is easier.*

Jeha dug her heels in and propelled herself, flying towards the main pavilion of the palace. She was cut short when another flying beast headed towards them. This one had a wingspan the length of five men and was twice the size of the others they'd fought.

*Caution,* she warned her sisters. *Danger.*

# TWO

# THE SENTINELS

## JEHA

Multiple waves of recognition and acknowledgement made her skin prickle.

With one gauntleted hand over her wound, she tucked the weapon under her armpit, tightly between the gambeson and her arm.

*Please*. Another request immediately granted by the Essence. New smoke threads enveloped her spear, and the weapon transformed into a tri-edged lance. If made of metal, it would have weighed far too much for Jeha to wield, but the smoke was weightless, making it her weapon of choice.

"Let's end this."

*Together*, her sisters said. Olon, Shakil, Helia. They darted towards the beast in a coordinated triangular formation. Their movements were smooth; practiced to exhaustion, to perfection. No room for failure. They were the Red Sun's sentinels after all.

The power of the smoke weapon burned her calloused palm. This wasn't the first time and wouldn't be the last. The Essence's gifts were meant to be cherished and difficult to attain. If she got what she wanted, the drawbacks were only fair.

The tri-edged lance was Jeha's best weapon, a harbinger of justice that punished those who dared threaten the peace of the Known World. With every swing of the blade, smoke threads trailed in its wake, seeping with the Essence. The flying monster was within reach. It looked as though a hungry beggar had its skin turn grey and grown bat wings, sharp fangs, and claws. There were patches of hair on its head, but there was nothing human about the creature other than its general shape. Jeha twisted the weapon and turned while paying attention to the beast's agile movements. She didn't have time for this dance of life and death when her duty called. This had to end quickly.

"We need to cut one of its wings," she roared. Gritting her teeth, she pushed forward with another blow. "If we do, it won't fly and our way will clear."

*Use me as bait*, Olon's voice sounded in her mind.

Jeha's panic mixed with the honour and respect she had for her sister's selfless bravery. She wouldn't defy her wish.

*Then go, Sister.*

Olon dove and approached from below, close to the rooftops. Jeha's heart wavered at seeing how close her battle sister had gone to one of the pavilion roofs. The beast looked down and changed course to crash into Olon from above. That distraction was the break Jeha needed. The demon might be fast, but Jeha was faster. She struck, but the swinging motion wasn't as fluid as it should be as her wound ached at the worst moment. Still, Jeha didn't buckle, gritting her teeth and carrying the pain as she went on.

She aimed her swing for the centre of the fiend's body. The tri-edged lance made a sound in her hand, and she swung it effortlessly. The beast noticed, but it was too late. The lance cut through its wing with little resistance. The beast snarled, but without a wing, it could no longer fly and crashed through a roof, a plume of dust rising in its wake.

"Thank you, Sister," Jeha said as she met Olon with a smile.

The squads of sentinels loomed well above the body of the flying beast. Jeha found it strange how the fiendish beings never turned into dust or ashes. She had always thought they'd just fade into darkness, but their bodies were always left behind. Actual bodies of flesh, bones, and skin. There didn't seem to be anything about them that indicated an external source of energy, which left her puzzled.

"Sister?" Olon asked.

She shook herself out of her thoughts. "Yes. Let us go. To the royal chamber."

She darted towards her destination, the battle sisters tailing in a tight formation. This time, there was no enemy or obstacle. She was so close to the heart of the Essence, she could feel a corruption working to seep into it, as though a parasite had stung her and was now injecting poison into her veins. The entire place reeked of death and otherworldly existence. She grimaced, and only the warm embrace of centuries-old sisterhood kept her resolve burning hot.

The palace was destroyed, its ancient beauty gone. In its stead, just ruins of smoke and ash, scattered debris and rubble, with dead bodies everywhere. Her eyes widened, and her heart skipped a beat as she took notice. It was sheer darkness. Perhaps only the Red Sun King could put an end to this mayhem now.

The giant oak gate that once stood at the entrance of the royal chambers now sported a large hole, burnt edges still hot.

No time to linger.

She jogged through the inside of the chambers and the Essence competed with the foul smell of the Deceiver. Jeha hoped it wasn't too late.

Her sisters flooded her with warmth as she made her way inside.

The once bright hallways were now devoid of light and the sconces that remained on the walls were dark. A chill ran through Jeha as she stepped onto the cold limestone floor. The royal chambers were not the lavish palatial quarters most people expected. The place had been built for breadth, with a focus on symmetry. Tree trunks made their way inside, and ivy and other plants Jeha didn't recognise clung to almost every wall. There was no more perfect place for the Essence and her avatar.

The more Jeha walked those halls, the more she sensed the overwhelming wrongness. The Deceiver's influence was so strong it almost made her retch.

"Help, please!" Maids and servants ran into hiding as soldiers of the Red Sun Army lay dead over the stones. The valiant ones had handled some of the hordes, but containing the breach had been impossible. Their corpses told the story of the gruesome battle they'd fought. Eyes torn from their sockets, missing limbs, and slit throats all too common among them.

It made Jeha sick. This should be impossible.

The battle sisters reached a broken door that led to the governing centre of Ushar and the royal quarters. In normal circumstances, she wouldn't be allowed in, but she was willing to risk punishment this time.

The Red Sun King's quarters were as magnificent as she'd expected them to be. White banners of the crimson Red Sun covered every wall. Depictions of old sentinels, smokesmiths, and other disciples of the Essence carved in stone statues reflected the moonlight that poured from the long windows. The silence worried Jeha, but the stench even more so. The Essence was guiding her to the source of all this mess. The Deceiver's new avatar was close. She had wondered who it could be. The empire wasn't perfect and neither were its people, but she just couldn't fathom anyone she knew being corrupted in such a way.

"Sister..." Olon started.

Jeha nodded. "I know."

A man stood across the stone bridge, just outside the door to the royal quarters. At first she couldn't see him, but she could smell the foulness oozing from him immediately. A prickle from the Essence whispered "danger" in her mind. This was the man, the Deceiver's avatar, the one responsible for the destruction of Ushar. Jeha struggled to settle her own fear. The Deceiver would never pick a weak avatar, so whoever this man is, he must be powerful.

She squinted as she approached carefully. He had shaggy blonde hair and lean features, and his dark gambeson was trimmed in silver.

*No, it can't be.*

General Agor of the Red Sun Army. This was the Red Sun King's blood brother.

*Ready yourselves*, she told the sisters.

General Agor wiped his gauntlet on the gambeson, blood staining the garment. He looked almost indifferent to his surroundings. Behind him was a trail of bodies—the very men he was supposed to lead.

"Is this really necessary?" The general's voice boomed like thunder, echoing along the hallway. "Walk back, sentinels."

Jeha bent her knees and clasped her tri-edged spear. Red Sun's brother or not, General Agor was corrupt. He was the source of the scourge. Jeha felt it now. Her sisters acknowledged and gave each other the Essence's power and might through the bond that connected them. Jeha thought about what she could say—tell him to step away from the door, to walk away, or surrender and accept punishment for his deeds—but that would yield no results. General Agor had fallen under the Deceiver's thumb. That much was clear. No man could come back from that.

*One for all.*

*And all for the Red Sun.*

Jeha charged at the general with her lance, carrying the might of the Essence. No hesitation. She swung, but the general was too fast. He dodged her strike with ease and unsheathed his sword in time to parry the strikes from her battle sisters. Countless blades came his way, and the man fended them off with his dark sword.

His sword flashed and he moved faster, parrying and then striking in a dance of steel and smoke. Agor's blade moved faster than Jeha's spear, matching the flurry of blows with ease. Jeha gritted her teeth and pressed forward. She swung the spear once. Twice.

She had been hoping to trap Agor's blade in the shaft of her tri-edged spear, but the general pulled the blade out. Jeha stepped back, but maintaining distance was hard when the man moved with the fury of a storm, his sword a whirlwind of death. Jeha's spear was long and moved quickly, but Agor was a man possessed.

He smirked.

He set his eyes on Sister Shakil and, in a flash, cut her in the ribs. The gambeson should have absorbed the blow, but like Jeha's spear, Agor's black sword was no ordinary weapon.

As Jeha stepped back again, Agor side-stepped, twirled on his heel, and ducked, then sprung up and targeted Shakil again. With a vicious thrust, his blade broke through the gambeson's weaved plate and the sister fell on her back, the wound too deep.

Pain flooded Jeha. Her own and her sisters'. A wave of sorrow and sadness ignited another spark of anger. It was hard to purge Ushar from the foul creatures that plagued it, but fighting one of her own was incomparably worse. She could try to rationalise why the general had decided to betray his family, the Usharian Empire, and the sentinels he should lead, but she would never have an answer. All she had was a void in her soul and a bitter taste in her mouth. It was almost wrong to turn her weapon against him, but it was revolting to see him end Shakil, once of her sisters. Jeha was never prepared for this kind of loss. It was like losing a limb, a part of herself that was gone, and a sorrow that multiplied many times over, shared and enhanced by the bond between the battle sisters.

She launched herself at him, swinging her spear, stabbing with the shaft and the butt alike, her feet barely touching the stone floor. Revenge wasn't the answer, but neither was meekness. She struck at his head. Then his chest. His hips and legs.

*Coordination.*

Her battle sisters understood. A coordinated assault, with two squads aiming at the legs and feet; others striking at his head and torso. Agor smirked again, seeing through their effort, jumping away before they got into position. Jeha struck, anticipating where he'd land. She'd expected his evasive manoeuvre and wiped the smirk off his face. Her blade found his thigh and cut deep.

Agor screamed with pain. He jumped back, but Jeha gave him no reprieve. Even with a useless thigh, he fought like no one Jeha had seen in centuries on the battlefield. All those elite sentinels doing their best to end him and still he survived. No... he *thrived*.

The resolve of her battle sisters was wavering and their frustration rising, she could tell. Agor parried three more strikes and moved alongside his dark sword towards her. Then he ducked and his sword found Sister Olon.

*No.*

Agor's blade pierced her plated gambeson. Olon dropped to her knees.

*No.*

A flood of grief overwhelmed Jeha, and the pain of all the sentinels who had lost another sister enveloped her. Her walls of emotionless duty were crumbling. Her body started trembling, and her breath caught. Her mouth was dry, and she was almost nauseous. Even for a sentinel like her this was overwhelming. She watched as Olon's body fell, lifeless. Centuries of life, devotion, and training, wasted at the whim of a blade and the corrupted man wielding it.

Jeha's courageous sister had gone to the underworld.

*How dare he?*

Pain and shock burst out of her in a fit of rage, and she swung the blade wildly at him, knowing well how dangerous it was. Jeha would make him pay. The sisters cooled her temper, but the hollowness remained. She *wanted* the rage to fuel her, not the tampered emotions of a dutiful sentinel.

Still, she thanked them for it. They never failed to give her hope. They could still defeat Agor and get to the Red Sun King. They could still help defeat the Deceiver.

They were the sentinels of the Red Sun.

The distraction of Olon's departure had earned Agor the chance to get some distance. The general closed his eyes and raised his right hand, then held onto something invisible in front of him and moved his hand to the side, as if he was peeling a giant, invisible onion. Light nearly blinded Jeha as he did so, wind and dust blowing from his direction. Jeha shielded her eyes from the gust and when she opened them again, a large ring of fire hung in the air, exuding foul energy.

*Another rift.*

A moving black mass emerged from the portal, filling her with dread. Two massive, grotesque hands of dripping darkness held onto the edges of the rift, and a ten-feet-tall demon squeezed itself through. With short legs and a much larger humanoid torso, the creature had a muscular build, arms covered with dark scales. A viscous substance coated its skin. Jeha's heart raced. It was as though she was choking on air. The creature was foulness made flesh. It couldn't be natural. She had to force herself to ignore her immediate instinct to flee. If she ran, who would stand there and fight it?

The heat emanated from the beast's body, and its eyes shone like two simmering coals staring directly at her.

Every bit of her body ached to run, her survival instincts kicking in.

"Sister? What should we do?" Sister Sohara asked.

Jeha hesitated. Her gaze shifted between the demon, the door that separated her from the royal quarters, and her battle sisters.

*This is what we fight for, sisters.*

"And we fight to the death." Sister Amel appeared from behind them, followed by the rest of them. Hope ignited in Jeha. They couldn't abandon their duty to protect the Red Sun King, nor each other.

"How good it is to see you." Jeha's eyes welled. "Thank you, Sister."

"Thank me when we're through that door."

Amel's gauntlet rested on her dented pauldron and only then did Jeha realise how tired she was. The Essence had been feeding her, providing her with all she needed: power, speed, strength, and resolve. How could she not give everything she had?

"It's a shame." Agor shook his head, then made for the door. "Your reputation precedes you, Jeha. It didn't have to end like this. I could have spared you."

The demon roared, and a heatwave blasted them as light emerged from his oesophagus.

"He's a Spitfire. Our weapons are useless," Sister Amel said with gritted teeth.

Jeha knew it to be true. It was useless to fight, but it was also too late to run. There was one thing left to try. If they were fast enough—lucky enough—they could run past the demon and avoid its blows and incoming fire.

She exchanged looks with her sisters. Together in life; together in death. That was good enough.

Jeha turned to Sister Sohara, the most recent addition to the sentinels. "You stay, Sister. If it's the end we're facing, then you shall honour our memory. Make sure our ways are not lost and forgotten. Then you'll be the heir to the sentinels."

Tears washed Sohara's face underneath her helm. She nodded.

*One for all.*

*And all for the Red Sun!*

Jeha shot towards the demon with the power of the Essence. With the strength of her sisters. Life or death, it didn't matter.

With her spear pointing towards the demon, she made for the door, following Agor, the traitor. As she neared the foul monster, light and heat consumed her.

*I'm sorry, Red Sun. I've failed.*

But she had no regrets.

A blend of molten purple rock and infernal fire engulfed her, making her one with the Essence.

# THREE

# THE DARKNESS

## AGOR

B ile rose in Agor's stomach as he closed the only remaining door to the inner chambers. Such a waste. Jeha was strong. She and the sisters had slowed him down more than he'd expected. He stood for a moment. Such a shame it had to be this way. And now the Palace of Brilliance lay in ruin.

*What a waste.*

On the other side of the thick gates, there was only misery as the sisters charged to their death with a war cry.

Then silence.

Agor let out a breath and allowed himself to take in how much chaos he'd caused in the city he loved, to the people he loved. There was blood splattered on all the pearly walls and polished floors. The expensive furniture was now ruined. All of it evidence of the Old One's fiends and their vicious doing. His doing.

He tried to avoid looking at it at first: the bodies of all the fallen guards, some still gripping their halberds even as they moved on to the underworld. His bile rose again. He hadn't killed those people himself, but he might as well have. He'd brought chaos with him the moment he opened the first rift.

Walking towards the inner chambers, Agor scanned the bodies of the fallen for familiar faces. His worst nightmare would be finding someone he'd known. An old squire, or maybe the master of arms. They were all supposed to protect Alamakar, after all.

The thought of facing his own brother, the Red Sun King, still left Agor apprehensive, but the Old One had left little room for doubt. His will had to be served. Everyone would call him the Deceiver, without realising they, themselves, were deceived by the Essence. Addicted to it. Poisoned by it. The entire world spun at the Essence's will, and the Old One was the only entity powerful enough to put an end to this shameless dependence.

Agor had called him the Deceiver too, once. He'd spoken the same drivel and drank from the Essence for far too long, but no more. Everything had become clear after the Old One showed him the unequivocal truth about the world and his place in it.

He shook off those thoughts and stopped looking for familiar faces or reasons to feel guilty about what he was doing.

He couldn't find any.

They had never listened to him, so all this had been an unfortunate necessity. He had tried killing as few of them as possible, but it seemed as though he had a target on his back of late.

He opened the door with his bloodied gauntlet. Inside the inner chamber were the usual simple decorations, with banners inlaid in golden line and the odd expensive portrait, but nothing extravagant, just as Alamakar liked it. Ah, the frugality of his brother... All his trees and vines climbing up the walls had made themselves at home there, much like the Essence had.

Agor bit his lip. He loved his brother. They'd always got along, and Alamakar had rewarded his counsel. In fact, his brother was the embodiment of justice and righteousness. He had just been... *consumed* by the Essence.

He heard clattering and grunts from the next room. Heavy boots stepped on stone where one of the Old One's friends—perhaps a Spitfire or a Lantern Horn—fought someone. But that deep in the royal chambers, it could only be one person.

Agor pushed the door open, ripping it off its hinges. He went in, and his eyes widened as he found his nephew Zerike struggling to fend off the mortal strikes of a Lantern Horn nearly twice his size. One confused young boy standing armed with a short sword against a creature that towered over even the tallest of men. An entourage of guards, servants, and courtiers lay dead in spreading pools of blood.

*No!*

Agor swooped in before real panic settled in him. With two strikes, he carved the Lantern Horn open, slicing his body in three parts. Zerike's eyes shifted between Agor and the fallen Lantern Horn. Agor rushed to comfort his brother's only heir with an arm around his shoulders.

Zerike looked as though he was about to cry. The boy had shaggy hair, not unlike Agor's, but his wiry frame made him look younger than his sixteen springs, and he stood at about half his father's height.

"It's alright, Zerike. It's alright. I'm here. Nothing will hurt you now."

Zerike looked at him, confused. Frustrated. Perhaps angry. Agor understood. He'd been that age before and it came with a sense of powerlessness, as though one's mind was developing faster than the body allowed.

"Thank you, uncle. You saved my life. I'm so glad you're here. Where is Father? Where is everyone else?"

"I'm sure your father is already on his way here."

Alamakar was the reason Agor was here, after all. His brother would sense his presence. He would sense the Old One just as Agor felt the power of the Essence dripping from every part of the palace, a toxicity he needed to purge. Alamakar should be deploying his Red Sun Army, controlling forces, and destroying the rifts, though Agor knew his brother would not allow his only son to be hurt. Not when he could feel such a real threat. He would soon arrive, and Agor would do what he needed to do.

"What is happening, uncle?" Zerike's voice trembled. "I don't understand."

Agor evaded the question. It was painful to see the boy in such a state. Many people would go their entire lives without experiencing such terror. "Come, nephew. Let us sit together. Let us calm ourselves."

Zerike didn't look as though he wanted to sit. He seemed restless, and his eyes never left Agor. "Uncle? Why... are you so calm? You look... peaceful."

Agor smiled, but pain shot through him. Guilt. Remorse. Both quickly squashed by the resolve of what he had to do.

Instead of answering, he shrugged, then sat at the window parapet. Looking outside, he observed the results of his own betrayal. He glanced back at Zerike, who was taking quick steps away from him.

Agor smiled, proud of who the man was becoming.

*Clever, clever boy.*

It made all of this so much worse than it had to be.

Just as Zerike was making a run for the door, Agor drew upon the Old One's power, lifted his arm, and made a fold in the threads that held reality together. These lines were invisible to everyone but him because the Essence hadn't corrupted them yet.

Pulling on the threads of time didn't quite stop time itself, but it made Agor momentarily faster than everybody else.

He drew another line in the air, pulled at the fold, and another rift opened. Zerike was left stagnant, moving but at such a slow speed it looked as though he had turned into a statue. This was Temporal Exploration, the reason he and the Old One stood a chance against the Essence and her minions.

Agor left his nephew and entered the rift. Even now, that journey was difficult, taking a toll on his body. Yet again, he found himself swimming in the infinite aether. Stars shone in the distance. Then he made for his destination: the same Known World he had come from, just at a different age. He wasn't sure how he knew to do this, or how he knew to navigate the infinity, but he had ever since the Old One had made him his avatar, lending him his strength and his wisdom in exchange for acting on his behalf. A good deal as far as Agor was concerned.

Everybody thought the rifts connected the Known World to other worlds—some even dared say the underworld—but Agor knew they also allowed someone to travel through time.

Agor floated in the nothingness until he stopped at an ancient time when beasts roamed the land. The memories of the Old One provided him the wisdom for it. It was as though a giant wave of knowledge flooded him. Most of them were memories he didn't recognise; of times and places he would never know. It was like walking in the world's largest library during an earthquake, and all the books were falling off the shelves and on top of him, even as he ran for cover. Still, within the torrent of memories, he found the ones he needed: those that showed the Old One battling the Essence in ages long past, their perpetual war longer than time itself. More importantly, he knew why they'd fought. The Essence insisted on infesting everything it touched, on controlling everyone with its blissful touch, and placing itself as a ruling deity, while the Old One was cast aside as her dark brother, the one with the touch of death.

Once again, Agor pulled on the invisible threads of reality that held time and space together and bridged the two rifts together, creating a portal. Then he slipped between times long past and went back to *his* time and to the Palace of Brilliance. Perhaps seeing the rift and the extent of his new power would make Zerike think twice about running away. Agor couldn't have that, not when there were so many creatures lurking in the palace.

After being the conduit for the Old One's power, how could he not feel anything but reverence? The name wasn't in vain. He had been around for a long time, multiple times over.

The rift was open now, covering the door that would allow the boy to leave. With a snap of his fingers, he was back in time.

Zerike stopped as soon as he saw the rift.

"You can't go. It's not safe outside this room." Agor faced the panicked eyes of his dear nephew. "Now, sit down, please. I insist."

Zerike's gaze could have bored holes into his face, but the boy accepted his request and sat at the parapet. Silent, yet defiant, he did not take his eyes off Agor. Truly, his father's son. Why did things need to be like this?

"Would you like to ask me any questions?"

Agor studied the boy, his eyebrows wrinkling above the nose bridge. There was wisdom in the youth. A certain rage bubbling beneath the surface. A willingness not to look away or show fear, but his furrowed brow betrayed him. Agor imagined the stampede of feelings lighting up the young man's mind. And yet, he barely showed anything. One day, he could be a good ruler to his people, though Agor wasn't sure that day would ever come.

"Why?" Zerike eventually asked, his voice dipping an octave. "*Why* did you do it?"

Agor's smile was faint. Of course, the boy had realised that *he* had done all of this. Where to begin?

"Because I had to. It may sound silly, but it's the truth. I had to do it."

The boy scowled, then pointed at the body of a servant not three paces away from where they sat. "Did you *have* to do that, too?"

"I saved you, didn't I?"

The boy stared at him and swallowed, but quickly found his resolve. "I matter very little if everybody dies. And everyone *is* dying. I want to know why."

"The world is complex, but people are simple. They're easy to corrupt."

"Do you speak of yourself, uncle?"

Agor soured and Zerike swallowed. "I didn't know you to be so insolent, nephew. We all corrupt easily, I suppose. But I'm talking about the Essence. The way she corrupts everyone. She has your father do her bidding, too. He's turned the entire Usharian Empire into a cult because of her and her power."

Zerike grimaced. "We *need* her power and you know it. We all do. My father is her avatar. How could you betray your kin, uncle? Your own brother..."

This was something Agor had pondered for decades. It wasn't a simple choice, but he was adamant.

"Family is important, nephew. I love you more than you think." Zerike scowled, but Agor didn't let that stop him. "And I love your father. But if the Essence continues to grow as it has, poisoning the minds and bodies of people, soon there will be no one left, only these vines, this ivy, and all that smoke. She feeds off of us, Zerike. This is overgrowth."

Zerike was dumbfounded, looking at him like the naïve youngster he was, mouth agape as though he couldn't choose between hatred and shame.

*Shame. What a bloody shame...*

"What is he promising you?" Zerike asked, eyes piercing him.

"Promising me? You think I do this for self-betterment?"

"You always envied my father."

Agor laughed, though the child was starting to ruffle his feathers. "Envied him? I would *never* seek to be in his shoes. Too many lives depend on him."

"And yet, you're the Deceiver's avatar, now."

"That's only the means to an end."

"What end, *uncle*?" Zerike spat that last word as though Agor hadn't carried him in his arms as a babe. Hadn't spent hours training him in combat, teaching him warfare, strategy, and court politics. "You say it's for the world, but it's for *you*. You've always hated being the shadow in the light that Father casts. So you found your own twisted way to grab power, to seize that light. You couldn't be the hero, so you're making up a delusional scenario in which you can force yourself to be one."

A surge of anger flared in Agor. The child was teasing him. He hadn't lived three hundred years to have an infant think he could spew whatever words he saw fit. And yet, Agor loved the boy. Even angry, Agor couldn't blame him. His father would soon join them, and once he did, he would have a difficult choice to make.

"I'll let you go when your father arrives. No need for you to die like the others. Not all hope is lost. You can lead men without the Essence."

"Fuck you!" the boy said.

"What did you—"

"Fuck. You." Zerike did not stutter. "I will not abide by your rules. I'm not a squire any longer. One day I'll be king and, should my father perish, I'll become the avatar in his stead. I won't rule without the Essence."

Agor snarled. "How wrong you are."

This was it. He had tolerated much and forgiven even more, but the boy's insolence was crossing all lines of propriety.

*Have I been too naïve? Dreaming of a peaceful future without the Essence?*

No, he simply saw what others couldn't see. He had sailed the aether, seen other worlds and other times. He simply *knew* things his people didn't.

"I've always hated you, you know?" Zerike said, eyes locked on him. "You are a petty man, thinking yourself above the rest. Even me. It's always about you being in charge. You being the master of arms. Everything you do has always been for yourself. Don't make up some faux noble cause. You're in it for your own gain. You're an easy, eager mind for the Deceiver to fool. I think my father knows it but he must pity you, because you're his brother. His twisted little brother. That's why he's kept you around so long—to keep an eye on you. I suppose he..."

Agor's gauntlet squeezed Zerike's neck, crushing his windpipe. All his love had been replaced by anger. A darkness rose within him. This was what he had suspected people thought of him, even when he was the better swordsman, the better general, or the most eloquent speaker. They all saw his darkness against Alamakar's light. No matter what he did, that's all they'd ever see. Perhaps that's what he really was.

"I suppose he failed, then."

Zerike's hands slammed into Agor's gauntlet, and he kicked and spun, trying to free himself. Too bad for him, Agor's grip would not waver. Where was the insolence now?

Then, Zerike made for Agor's scabbard and, in a last, desperate move, took hold of the sword hilt before Agor could stop him.

"No! Don't!" Agor screamed, getting a hold of himself. It was too late. The sword, *Timeless*, had been an ancient gift from the Old One, meant only for him to wield, and now Zerike's palm was wrapped around it.

*No!*

No one but Agor could wield it. More than a sword, *Timeless* was an artifact, or a conduit through which Agor could manipulate the course of time. Zerike didn't have that ability. The boy's face went pale, and he froze as he slowly became lost to time, even after Agor rushed to remove the sword from his hand. Agor shook him, but he stayed like that, unmoving as though paralysed.

It was already too late to save the boy. Agor cursed himself. The foolish child thought he could kill Agor with his own blade. Agor should have never made that mistake.

*I'm as foolish as he is.*

Zerike had become trapped in time. Then his eyes lost focus, and he stopped moving entirely.

"No!" Agor screamed, then his squeal turned into a quiet mourn. He cupped his nephew's beardless face, and flinched upon realising it was now solid as a rock. "No..."

He cursed both himself and the Old One.

His poor nephew. He had tried to choke him. And for what? For saying things young people say when cornered?

He shook the boy's paralysed body, but it was as though made of stone. His heartbeat was faint. What could Agor do? He had never intended for this to happen. Perhaps the Old One...

"Do something!" he yelled.

*ME? IT'S YOU WHO DOES MY BIDDING, AGOR.*

# FOUR

# TIMELESSNESS

## AGOR

Shivers ran down Agor's spine. Even as the Old One's avatar, it was still a thrill to be spoken to by him. The depth of his knowledge lived in Agor, but the Old One had a mind of his own and power he scarcely shared. Agor couldn't see a man of flesh and bone, but it was as though he did. His shape and size were blurry, but the power oozing from him was overwhelming. Humbling.

Still, Agor had to try. He fell to his knees and interlocked his fingers.

"Please... He didn't know better. He was my nephew. You can bring him back."

The Old One responded in his mind, as always. "Why? I live in and out of time but matters of life and death are for my brother, not me. This day has fate written all over it, Agor. Can't you feel it? There is no more hiding. No more running. We've freed the Lantern Horns again. Now, my sister will come, and with her we will either perish or end this forever. Our clash will be remembered for thousands of years. We shall face our worst fears, but we know we are only doing what must be done. Nieces and nephews matter little when we have so much else to worry about. Don't you agree?"

"Yes," Agor said. He was unsure why he'd said it so promptly, and also unsure why he was surprised he'd said it. It made sense. The Old One knew things. Everything.

The Old One knew best.

But the pain of Zerike's demise hadn't gone away. It sank deeper into Agor's heart, darkening it. He let out a lone tear. The one sign of pain and the weakness he couldn't hide. Of his humanity. It escaped him like a fleeing prisoner.

"Now, now, boy." There was jest in the Old One's booming voice. "No need to get emotional over something so trivial. You did what I asked, didn't you? The rifts are open. That should be enough to allow our friends to make their way here. And, more importantly, enough to get your brother's attention."

"Why not ambush him?" Agor shook his head. "Them."

"My sister spreads her seeds far and wide but her presence is best felt here, at the heart of the empire."

Agor walked over to the parapet overlooking the empire's capital. There was a solemnness in the Old One's voice. Was he getting nostalgic? Then self-hatred coursed through Agor and he abandoned the window, facing the trees and vines wrapping themselves around the marbled walls, the Old One guiding his mind.

"See? She's a plague... Still spreading day after day."

With a wave of his hand, the Old One's power flowed through Agor and the vines withered. Slowly, the trees hardened and turned to dead wood, shedding their leaves. Forever winter had befallen them.

Many accused the Old One's touch of bringing death, but it was just the passage of time, a natural and necessary correction to the Essence's wrongdoings. A beautiful thing it was, making time pass quicker for something that had no right to have been growing and festering, taking over everything. Passing so quickly, it jumped straight to the end of its life. It was what separated the Old One from His sister. When there was famine and disease, the Essence allowed it to grow. The Old One was capable of putting an end to it.

It almost allowed Agor to forget about Zerike. His lifeless body turned into a statue of flesh and bone. Agor forced himself to look away, grimacing.

The city he'd sworn to protect, being destroyed so it could be rebuilt. His family divided with his nephew dead. By his sword. It was all for a purpose, he knew. Still, a flood of emotions overpowered him. All the hatred he'd felt over the years. The love for his family, for his soldiers; even for the people he had led. All his pride had now been lost, his fears running ever rampant and a sadness looming over him. He knew life was hard, just had never felt it so ruthlessly.

No history to preserve, no family legacy to maintain. Agor wiped away his tears, took a deep breath, and gripped his sword's hilt. If the world was going to change, then that would be for the best. And he would be there to deliver it. To make sure of it.

*I'm ready for you, Brother.*

## FIVE

# THE SMOKE

## MATALA

The deafening roar of a distant creature rang in Matala's ears as he removed a handful of herbs from his belt pouch. He doused the leaves with a good bit of belleaf oil and, with shaky hands, spilled more than his masters would approve.

For the gods, it reeked! The entire world stank! Matala could hardly concentrate.

He blew on the oily herbs and they caught fire, as did anything doused in belleaf oil. Gentle flames consumed the herbal leaves and produced a thread of smoke which kept on growing. Matala brought the burning herbs close to his nose and took a deep whiff of their smoke. It burned his lungs first. It always did. Then it powered him up.

*Finally.*

The power he sought was upon him. Strength, speed, and an addictive sense of invincibility, which his masters always cautioned was an illusion. Matala felt invincible alright, but there was no such thing in the front lines. He was a bloody apprentice too, and this was the first invasion since he'd joined the Red Sun Army. Even with the smoke enhancing him, he couldn't stop his legs shaking at the sight of the bloody creatures in the distance and the bodies they left in their wake.

*I must be the most cowardly Smoke Rider in the garrison.*

The other smokesmiths and Smoke Riders from his garrison readied themselves, their faces lit by flames as they blew on their greasy herbs. All around them, towering demons spewed fire, burning Ushar to the ground. He'd never seen anything like it. Other garrisons scrambled to organise across the burning city, attempting to defeat the otherworldly invaders.

Matala, of all people, was among those meant to put an end to it.

"What are you doing, boy? There are demons everywhere. People are counting on us!" Master Dugala's voice was raspy, rusted by years of breathing smoke.

Matala nodded and joined the rest of his squad, begging every god alive or dead to help him hide his shaking legs well enough from Master Dugala.

They raced through the streets of Ushar like they owned the bloody place—no alley and street was a mystery to them.

With smoke in their lungs, sprinting was easy work, so Matala took long, effortless strides as they raced to engage two creatures. They were far too big for how fast they moved. Smoke-enhanced blood filled his veins as his heart pumped at thrice the normal speed, infusing Matala with the Essence's power. He was truly blessed to be a smoke-smith, but he'd gone beyond that and become a Smoke Rider too.

Matala was the first man in the garrison's charging line. The youngest and newest were always sent first—an opportunity to show their worth, the masters said. *Or to die if they have none.*

The smoke helped, and Matala found his nerves fading as he charged one of the creatures, but he was still a coward, always a coward. He shook all the worries out of his mind. The pressure to perform for his master and his garrison disappeared. It was just him and that mountain of a beast now, with its muscular shoulders and spikes. Matala produced a flask of belleaf oil and doused himself with it.

Flames covered Matala, turning him into a human fireball.

He was on fire.

He screamed in pain. An immense heat consumed his skin, hair, and everything else that wasn't bone.

The first few times had been unbearable, but Matala didn't pass out from shock anymore, and the smoke he breathed kept the pain tame. Around him, his comrades did the same. Amid roars and howls of pain, each Smoke Rider turned into a ball of fire and light, screaming and cursing at the demons that forced them to go through this self-mutilation.

Like a snake shedding its skin, Matala's flesh quickly burned to ashes, leaving only his skeleton enveloped in a thick, dark smoke that wouldn't leave him. It was cathartic to sever ties with the world of the living, to lose his body and turn himself into an undead skeleton.

It was as though he had been liberated.

Unleashed.

That wasn't quite true—he would still go back to being human—but there was a lightness to turning undead and riding the smoke like a ghost floating in the wind.

"All hail the Dousers!" howled Master Dugala at his side, also a skeleton.

"All hail!" he shouted back.

Matala was wind, air, smoke, and death, just like the rest of the Dousers. For the gods, he was proud to be in this elite unit! If only he wasn't so cowardly, he could accomplish great things.

Now one with the herbal smoke, Matala shaped the fumes and let them curl around his fist. The smoke expanded and moulded itself into an enormous, two-edged claymore as light as air.

He had summoned the bloody smoke sword, but how in the world would he fight that beast? How could Master

Dugala let him go first in the front lines? Expectation weighed heavily on his shoulders. Matala couldn't afford to fail, but he was already buckling under the pressure.

The behemoth spat bursts of lava across Ushar and created rock formations where houses had been. Matala locked his gaze on the demon, then followed his instinct. He swung the smoke blade in strong, quick blows. First overhead, then sideways. He might not be able to take to the sky like the sentinels, but being himself should be good enough.

The smoke claymore bit into the monster's heel and the beast roared, noticing him. The other Dousers surrounded the demon with their own weapons, slashing at its leathery skin. There were more of the monstrous giants on the way, though. The bloody capital was riddled with them, so Matala knew his mates wouldn't be able to stay.

"This one is yours. Kill it and head to the western rift. It must be closed or destroyed. We're going to deal with the incoming horde," Master Telafa shouted as he and the other Dousers went on ahead.

Matala looked at the demon, taller than any building in Ushar. *Kill it? Just kill it. Yes, I'll do that, of course. Easy.*

Master Dugala buried his smoke blade deep in the demon's calf, then jumped back to dodge a blow that made the earth shatter. "Well, you heard him."

Matala swallowed and took a step back. "What a day," he said.

The monster was irate now, shooting fiery gravel towards them with every step. It swung its arms and crashed its fists into the ground, destroying buildings and everything else.

"Come on, Matala. Don't you see it? The city needs us. The sentinels are bound to protect the Red Sun King, so only *we* can close the rifts. You have been trained for this. You're ready."

Matala nodded and did his best to remember his training. *I'm just a bloody apprentice.* It was hard to concentrate when he'd never been in this situation before. When the city he'd grown up in burned like an enormous bonfire fit for gods and demons. When he hadn't trained for *this,* and somehow he—*HE*!—was supposed to stop it from happening. *Bloody sack of shit.*

Matala took another whiff of the smoke to keep his undead transformation intact. His lungs would hurt afterwards, and... why did he keep thinking about this? It was a bloody battle!

*I need to focus.*

He let his sword grow and the smoke carry him, imagining he was a leaf floating in a hurricane. No, that *he* was the hurricane. The sword kept growing and Matala shot to the side to evade the demon's molten rock shower. He let the smoke claymore soften and willed it to take the shape of a rope or a whip. Only Smoke Riders could manipulate smoke like that. A gift from the Essence.

Carried by the southern wind, he dodged four wild swings from the angry demon, calculated the timing, and threw the smoke whip again, looping it around its neck.

"Master!" He held the demon's neck in a tight choke-hold. The creature battled against it, but his claw-laden paws were much too large to unwrap the smoke whip.

Master Dugala stuffed his smoke blade in the demon's golden eye, then again in the other eye. The creature howled in pain. He let go of the hold, and the demon crashed and fell to its death.

Matala stared at the dead behemoth, and Master Dugala patted him on the shoulder. Was he acknowledging him? Matala couldn't tell.

They'd done it, though! *I've done it!* It hadn't been impossible after all.

"Let's keep going to the western rift."

In the sky, the sister sentinels of the Red Sun Army engaged in aerial combat with creatures that would give Matala nightmares for a year. Weapons clashing and surges of power pulsed across the sky. The streets of Ushar were filled with the blood of the fallen citizens and the slain invaders brought over by the Deceiver. The southern wind drove whatever foul smell plagued the city towards the Palace of Brilliance.

Matala and Master Dugala rushed to the westernmost gate, where scout reports had pegged the rift. Without warning, a large fire broke out in front of them, blocking their path. Matala shielded his face, then hesitated, expecting a demon to follow the explosion. Instead, a pair of Smoke Riders appeared, also in their undead form.

"Who are you?" one asked.

"Captain Dugala of the Dousers. And you?"

"Oh! Apologies, Captain. We were told to head to the western—"

Before the man could finish his sentence, he and his companion collapsed under a pile of molten rock spat out by another demon that was following them. Extreme heat was followed by the demon standing in front of them, causing the ground to shake.

"No!" Matala cried.

Master Dugala pulled him back as three more horned beasts followed the Smoke Riders' trail. Those had been two of his mates. Hollowness filled his chest as he struggled to contain his horror and fear. *I can't do this. I can't do any of this.*

"The rift is our priority. Let's keep moving."

"Yes, master."

Matala was numb, only going through the motions. He'd seen death before, but never anything so foul and gratuitous. The city reeked of whatever it was that the demons produced. These two Smoke Riders could not just be fodder. He wouldn't accept that. They were people with passions and loved ones. With an aching heart drenched with sorrow and fear seeping into his mind, he followed Master Dugala.

*I'm a coward.* "I can't do this, master."

He regretted those words as soon as he spoke them.

Master Dugala turned to face him. "You can and you have. And you will. Do not let their deaths be in vain."

"How do I find the strength?"

"Find it? You bloody unleash it!"

His master's words were meant to be comforting, but he felt only anguish. He'd *wanted* to be a Smoke Rider. He'd been thrilled to be recruited into the Dousers. The most promising apprentice in decades, they'd called him. How wrong they had been. Now he was running from the demons, leaving two mates behind. A coward.

Master Dugala stopped and pulled him to the side. "Listen to me, boy. Snap out of it! Without us, the city is doomed. You've bloody done it. You killed that demon, which means you're no longer my apprentice. That means you've graduated to a real Douser now, so act like one!"

The turmoil in Matala would have yielded tears of sadness and joy if he wasn't a skeleton of smoke. A hint of pride settled next to the fear, balancing it.

He didn't *feel* like a real Douser, but he would have to trust Master Dugala.

He nodded. "Yes, master."

"I'm not your master anymore. Just Dugala."

Matala swallowed. "Thank you."

"All hail the Dousers, boy," Dugala said, his bony hand on Matala's skull.

"All hail!"

They continued through cobbles and rooftops alike, sailing in the smoky air like ships pulled by the wind. The rift was near. He could feel it pulsing. On the way there, though, Matala saw the explosions and heard the deathly screams of city-dwellers. A lady ran from a beast that latched onto her neck and snapped her in half. The building that used to host the imperial mint collapsed, the stones and mortar that made up the structure crumbling onto the roads like sandcastles. On top of the old building stood a roaring Spitfire, busying himself by dousing the entire street with volcanic magma from which both cobblers and carpenters had to run.

"We've never had an invasion like this."

"The Deceiver is back. If I was a betting man, I'd wager he's found himself a new avatar. A powerful one, by the looks of it."

Dugala *was* a betting man, and he almost never lost.

Matala could hardly believe it. Fear gained ground within him and smothered what tiny bits of bravery he had left. Fighting a monster with his mates was one thing, but battling entire hordes led by the Deceiver's new avatar was... something else entirely.

As they pushed toward the rift, a glimmer of light from his side of the road caught his eye. An orange glow was building on a street corner up ahead, the sure sign of a Spitfire preparing to release more gravel. Matala rushed to pull Dugala's arm, halting his forward progress.

"Fire incoming! Take cover!" Matala took another whiff of the smoke and slid between Dugala and the demon, the smoke sword growing in his hand.

Sure enough, the Spitfire edged round the corner, and his blast came without mercy.

Springing towards the creature, Matala jumped and willed his weapon to transform. The herbal smoke unravelled and shifted into a massive, round shield that could have protected five men.

That would do.

Matala leaned against the shield with his shoulder and pushed as gravel hit his newfound protection, like a thousand fists knocking on a single door.

*I will not lose Dugala too. I will not lose another mate.*

When the rocks stopped battering the shield, he let it puff back into wild smoke and rode it to Dugala. The demon was still there, with its horns and lizard-like skin.

"Matala... that was... Where did you learn that?"

*Does he mean the shield?* "I don't know. I just *thought* about it and it appeared."

Dugala hesitated. "I hope one day you realise your worth, boy. Let's go."

They turned to circumvent the demon, but it appeared before them, blocking their way to the rift. With a swing of its long tail, it sent them crashing against buildings and into debris. Matala saw red, then his vision blurred. A rush of smoke kept him going, unable to feel the pain. But the damage would come back later, when he stopped breathing the smoke.

*How can it move so fast? It's the size of a bloody castle.*

The demon didn't hesitate. Didn't falter. It pressed on; amber eyes locked on them. Dugala was up again as well, an oversized broadsword of smoke growing in his fist. Matala willed for his claymore again, and it dutifully appeared. They rushed to meet the demon and cut it down once and for all, but another swing of its arms caught Matala in the chest, sending him flying against a burning building. Another orange glow appeared in the demon's mouth. At the same time, a fissure tore the ground beneath them, rocks and dirt splitting.

*What a bloody day.*

Every time he tried to charge the demon, something was in his way. Even floating in the air and carried by the smoke, he wavered and tumbled, slamming against another building. "Are you all right?"

"Aye." Dugala sounded raspy. The smoke was taking its toll. "For now, I am. Tomorrow, I'm pretty sure I won't be."

Matala dragged himself up, thinking of those who hadn't survived the invasion. Those who would still die because of it. He might be an undead skeleton now, but

Dugala was right. There would be bruises, gashes, and scratches all over his human body tomorrow. His lungs would ache as though they were on fire, and he would be lucky to wake up before a day or two. The transformation was only a delay of the inevitable, but that gave him something nobody else had: time.

Summoning his smoke claymore again, he rushed the demon just as the shower of molten gravel hit him. Each impact shook the ground, and Matala raced between them, jumping, side-stepping, and ducking his way towards the demon.

Then he stuck the tip of the sword on the broken ground and willed it to grow, using the momentum to propel himself forwards, directly at the demon. Light as a feather, he slashed the beast, which used its forearms for protection. Each blow cut deep into its leathery skin, but no blows were close to being fatal. Dugala emerged behind him with his broadsword, swinging at the demon's shoulder. The fiend roared.

Matala used Dugala's distraction to cover himself in smoke. His claymore grew yet again. Now enveloped in smoke and its power, he pointed it at the demon's torso and stabbed with all his might. The hard skin resisted the blow at first, and despite the pain it caused, it was no killing strike.

# Six

# Cowardice

## Matala

"Aim for the neck, boy."

Matala dodged an arm swing from the beast, and the thundering sound of its giant fists hitting the ground nearly deafened his ears. He roared back at the demon and swung his smoke blade against it. The monster swatted it away as though Matala was an annoying insect.

*Damn it. I'm too bloody weak.*

Then he realised it wasn't about strength, but strategy.

"Wait for the next time he spits the gravel," he shouted to Dugala. "I'll distract him and protect myself with the shield. You sneak in from the side and slit its throat."

Dugala nodded and rushed to the right of a destroyed building. Matala distracted the demon with blows to its legs and torso, and eventually the orange glow came again. He prepared his smoke shield.

From the corner of his eye, he saw Dugala charge towards the demon, his broadsword beside him. But the gravel shower never came. The demon must have seen the glimmer of Dugala's smoke sword against the firelight and turned its attention on him.

*No.*

Matala charged forwards as fast as he could, his shield shifting back to the shape of his claymore.

*No.*

The demon spat rocks at Dugala. Matala watched in horror as Dugala was hit by multiple flaming boulders.

*NO!*

He finally reached the demon and swung the smoke blade in fury, catching the demon in its neck and spilling steaming blood. The demon held on, covering his wounded neck with one hand while the other sought to squash Matala.

*No!*

With nothing but rage and dark dread, he slashed at the demon, swinging his blade and stabbing at the neck in a flurry of strikes. The beast howled in pain until it buckled and dropped to its knees. With one last stab at the demon's face, Matala sent the foul creature down to the ground.

He rushed to find Dugala in the rubble, his legs covered in rocks that glowed orange, heat pulsing from them. His old master and friend was back in human form. His stubble was peppered with white hair and blood flowed from the corner of his mouth. His heaving chest denounced his troubled breathing, and his legs were likely burning and crushed under the rocks.

"I'm still alive, boy. Don't you worry about me. It takes more than that to get rid of old Dugala."

"Shh, don't speak. I'm taking you back to base."

Dugala shook his head. "No, you're going to the rift. You'll destroy it."

"Then you're coming with me."

"I can't move and you can't carry me."

"Yes, I bloody can!" Matala shouted. "We'll do it together."

"No, boy." Dugala's voice was hoarse. He stopped to swallow, more blood flowing from the corner of his mouth. His words were slurred. "Listen. You've got to show up for yourself, you hear me? Wake up every day and show up for yourself. If you don't, nobody will."

Matala shook his head as guilt and pain poured in. "What are you talking about? We need to get out of here."

"Show up, boy. Show up. I'm going to sleep now."

"Wait, Dugala. No." But it was too late. He was still breathing but had fallen unconscious.

Matala wanted to scream and burst into flames again. He didn't know if Dugala would die, but this was senseless. Even if he lived, his lungs would simmer for days. His body would take too long to recover, and he would probably die days later. Powerlessness washed over him.

He couldn't save Dugala, just as he hadn't been able to save the other Smoke Riders. Even if he saved a few dozen people, thousands more would still die.

Just as he was about to let himself collapse, he remembered Dugala's words.

*Show up for yourself.*

He could still *try* to do something. Try not to be a bloody coward. Every soul he saved would be a victory.

*I can try to close the rift.*

He shut his mind and put a lid on the sorrow that threatened to overtake him. Then he strode away from his master. It still hurt to leave Dugala helpless, prone to being put out of his misery by another demon, but Matala had a purpose. A mission. He took off.

Moments later, he spotted the large blue portal that broke the sky open. A portal that connected the Known World to whatever place this horde of demons called home. The edges of the rift were blue flames, like lightning. There were still creatures pouring out in droves, all much smaller than the behemoths he'd faced, but the numbers were not in his favour. He spotted about a dozen Smoke Riders facing the beasts, backed by squads of smoke-smiths.

Racing through the city, Matala made his way to the defenders. Balls of fire and waves of power exploded, and smoke surrounded them.

"How do we destroy the rift?" Matala had never done such a thing.

One of the smokesmiths noticed him and shrugged. "We have to get to it, and that's proving a pain. There's no end to these fiends."

Matala studied the rift and the rubble. The smokesmiths had set up what looked like a siege of the rift, doing their best to move forward and gain ground. The problem was that during sieges, the besieged would go hungry and yield or allies would come to help. With the rift, the beasts would just keep coming. It was an impossible fight for anyone trying to contain it.

Matala had an idea. They were close to the westernmost gate. Archers stood atop the wall and shot arrows at the demons.

"Let me try something." The smokesmith didn't respond. Maybe he didn't hear him. "Hey, I have a plan. Move your garrison to the right. I'm going to climb the wall."

"The wall? What in the world are you going to do there?"

"Just trust me," Matala nearly begged. "You've got to trust me. Can you please move your squads to the right?"

The smokesmith frowned.

"I'm Smoke Rider Matala of the Dousers unit. I have orders to destroy this rift."

Hundreds of them were too late to realise their peril as the stones crashed on top of them. Riding on the success of his first hit, Matala bellowed in victory and repeated the strike, faster than the first time. He put his entire body on that blow. Rocks fell and the demons below scattered.

He caught the eye of the smokesmiths.

*I'm not a coward now.*

Trying to prove just that, he leaped out of the battlements and towards the rift, wielding the mighty hammer. He had no idea how to destroy it. Could a smoke weapon do it? He'd find out soon enough.

Jumping, he swung the battle hammer and aimed at the rift's sparkling blue edge. This was the single hardest thing Matala had ever done. Despite the rush of the fight, he tensed up, his grip on the weapon tightening even more. That swing carried pain and hardship. It carried the hopes and fears of his mates and all the citizens who had just lost their homes and their sustenance. Matala allowed himself to be angry on their behalf, for rage to fuel him with reckless strength.

*I won't fail.*

The smoke hammer connected with the rift, and light blasted as though the sun had descended on the Known World. But Matala didn't let go of the weapon. He held it tight and, even blinded by the surge of light, he let the power of the blow ripple through his entire body. Matala wondered if that was what being hit by lightning felt like.

As the Essence's power collided with the rift, the light illuminated the skies and shockwaves of power hit his body, forcing him to finally let go of the hammer.

He was blinded and hurt. That blow had demanded everything he had, but he was sure the rift was gone. It had to be gone. Was it gone? He couldn't tell: he couldn't even see where he'd fallen in the aftermath of his assault on the rift.

He was dizzy, tired and, worst of all, exposed. If there were any demons around, they'd surely come after him, and he had no way of defending himself. He had given his all.

Then something—or someone—touched him. Warm hands enveloped his back, his neck, and the back of his head.

"You crazy bastard. You did it." The vaguely familiar voice sounded distant. Dugala? No, that couldn't be. Somebody else he knew. It didn't matter.

Matala still couldn't open his eyes, but the touch told him he was in his human form. And he would now pay the price of every bit of power he had used. With all the strength he still had, he wished for Dugala to live. For his accomplishment to mean something. For the Red Sun King to stop the Deceiver once and for all.

# SEVEN

# THE KING

## ALAMAKAR

Alamakar sat cross-legged in the wide, grassy temple with eyes closed, watching over the beautiful city of Ushar. With the Essence as his eyes, he felt the very core of the capital plagued by devils. It had been a mistake to veil his presence. His sentinels must be trying to find him.

Only a new avatar could have brought so much peril to the world.

Still with eyes closed, Alamakar resisted the pull of the Deceiver. This wasn't the first time Ushar had been attacked by the Deceiver and his minions. As much as Alamakar wanted to take the city's defence into his own hands, he had his purpose.

He delved deeper into his Inner Flight, widening the scope of what he could see through the Essence. She had told him not everyone could *feel* all the emotions of others. That was why she'd picked him to be her avatar—because he was good at bearing pain. Not because of his conquests, or his fearlessness. Not honour or courage, as many thought. Alamakar was exceptionally good at suffering.

And more of it awaited him, not that he was done cultivating the Essence's power, priming it into his body, preparing to fight.

He floated to his feet and opened his eyes, abandoning the Inner Flight. Without the all-seeing eyes of the Essence that the Inner Flight provided him with, using only his actual vision was a disappointment. Everything felt short-sighted, or almost incomplete.

*I'm going, Mother.*

*Yes, you are,* the Essence said. *I shall guide you.*

*There is no need. I know where to go.*

*For what you have in strength, you have twice as much in stubbornness, Alamakar. Why would you deny me?*

Alamakar walked to the exit of the temple, looking for his sentinels. The marble was covered in moss, vines and ivy climbing up from floor to ceiling, just as he liked; just green enough to allow the Essence to thrive.

*What kind of king would I be if I obeyed your every suggestion?*

*Suggestion? I issue commands and you heed them, boy.*

*And if I don't?*

Alamakar took the Essence's lack of response for resigned acceptance. She was the one who had provided for Ushar and allowed him to grow his empire, but he wasn't foolish. His loyalty was with her, but also with his people. She wasn't used to having her words denied, but she didn't seem to mind it much when he did.

Before he exited the temple, he picked up his scabbard and buckled it around his waist. Outside, the world was a nightmare. Devilish shrieks echoed in the distance and roars were followed by screams. His people. With no time to mourn the already heavy losses, Alamakar was ambushed by a group of shadowlings—the ones with the illuminated horns. They were powerful creatures, with bulging muscles and grey scales like fish. They snarled at him as they rushed him with sharp claws.

A trickle of fear grew within him. Just how deep into the city were these creatures? He shook it off, clasped the sword hilt, and unleashed *Red Perennial*. Alamakar floated like a feather and dodged the shadowlings' strikes as his heavenly blade cut through them. The crimson sword was tinted with the blood of slain kings and queens from ages long past.

The shadowlings came like waves crashing against a ravine, hitting at Alamakar mercilessly, a flood of claws and fangs aiming for his head and neck. Normally, he wouldn't bother with the creatures, but this time, they forced him to stoically repel them one by one, blow by blow with the blade. They weren't organised like soldiers, a savage frenzy possessing them. And there were so many of them. He wasn't afraid—he could handle them—but if the entire city was filled with them...

He leapt into the air and stayed there, first to avoid the rampage of demons that gnarled and jumped trying to reach him with their claws, and then to see the full extent of this invasion. It was even worse than he'd thought—this was no ordinary invasion.

One of the creatures managed to reach him, grabbing his ankle and trying to pull him back down. Alamakar gritted his teeth, firmed his grip on *Red Perennial*, and sliced the fiend with no spare thought, the demon's grip immediately loosening. Glancing down at the enormous pool of demons underneath him, he sighed. There was only one thing to do.

He embedded himself in the Essence.

Alamakar closed his eyes, dove into his Inner Flight, and became able to *see* again. He clutched one of the threads in the Essence's web around Ushar, the one connecting him to the web. He tore it apart and immediately felt the power of the Essence flowing in his veins. This was only a fraction of it, but plenty more than he needed to handle these demons.

Summoning the power, he charged the creatures and hit them with an energy blast that reduced them all to bits before landing on the cratered ground. Everything in a large circumference around him was reduced to dust.

*You can never resist making a show of it, can you?*

Alamakar grimaced. *You speak as though you don't like it.* He knew she couldn't argue with that.

Suddenly, pain burned across his back and Alamakar turned around to see a much larger shadowling. He cursed himself as the Essence chuckled in his mind. He'd missed one.

Alamakar tapped into the Essence again. She was there, always there, even when she was mad at him. She *was* the city, spreading through trees, grass, ivy, and the canals built purposefully to allow her growth. But where his connection to the Essence was always bright, as though a ball of fire pulsed inside him as her conduit, those flames of power that strengthened the Essence's web of influence were dim within him. The ball of fire was now but embers as she had to focus on repelling the invaders.

He'd better put an end to this before even more of the city was destroyed. Channelling his might through *Red Perennial*, he stabbed the creature and swung the blade upwards, slicing it in half. Another shadowling had closed the distance, approaching with its flickering horn. Alamakar swung *Red Perennial* again, and the blast of power from the blade alone was enough to send the beast crashing into a marble wall.

Flexing his legs, Alamakar jumped. He had no time for this. He could sense a foulness, as though the Deceiver's latest pawn was goading him. Who had he picked this time?

There were fewer shadowlings in the air, save for those with bat-like wings, their eyes shining.

Unlike the sentinels, he didn't need to ask the Essence for permission to use her powers. She needed him, a physical vessel for her growth and expansion, as much as he needed her for her power in ruling the world. Right now, he needed to fly. He surveyed the damage. The Zeiram Bastion looked compromised already, its left section burned, but he couldn't see any of the sentinels. Had all the battle sisters fallen? No, that couldn't be… Their role was to protect him, and they would head to where they thought he would be…

His eyes widened as he realised where they'd go.

The royal chambers. That's where they would head.

He cursed himself. If he only hadn't escaped them for a few moments of meditation. His sentinels were bound to protect him, but he was tired of being followed wherever he went, and now his sole step outside the kingdom's protocol had resulted in him being separated from his sentinels, who probably didn't know where he was. It was his fault for having sought peace. He should have known kings couldn't afford it.

He swallowed. The royal chambers were also the source of the stench carried in the air. A smell of rot and death so intense he wouldn't be surprised if it was poisonous, too. It wasn't an unpleasant smell like shit or piss, but it was *wrong* and unnatural, something that had no place in this world. And that's where his sentinels were going. That's where his family was supposed to be. His son...

*Zerike...*

The wound in his back flared like a bonfire with every movement, but it would heal. Groaning, Alamakar made sure there were no more shadowlings around. Gritting his teeth, he began to fly over Ushar, the wound affecting his balance. Where were his sentinels?

The white marbled buildings were in ruin. Smoke from the smokesmiths and Smoke Riders defending Ushar blended with that of the burning houses and markets and wheel wagons. Crimson covered sections of the cobbled streets. The blood of his people.

The Old One would pay for this.

*Not too eager, Alamakar. You mustn't be blinded by anger.*

He knew the Essence was right.

As he made his way to the royal chambers, the stench of foulness strengthened. It was like a swamp seeping into his nostrils, impossible to wave off.

A massive roar echoed in the night as yet another battle horn sounded from the northernmost watchtower. Another breach. Another compromised wall.

"My King! Red Sun!" Alamakar looked for that voice in the darkness. Poonama, one of his sentinels, was trying to fend off two bat-like devils twice her size. "The battle sisters were compromised. They went to the royal chambers.

Nothing good awaits them there. I was meant to protect you, but—"

Alamakar rushed to aid her, but before he could, one of the shadowlings' fists hammered Poonama's head and she lost consciousness, falling from the sky. Another shadowling crushed her with his claws.

As the sentinel hit the ground, Alamakar gritted his teeth and swallowed. Sentinels were powerful, but they shouldn't die because of his mistakes. And yet they still did.

The creatures turned to Alamakar as he looked at Poonama's lifeless body. She and her battle sister had sworn to protect him. They'd been raised together. They'd been accepted by the Essence too. Then he looked at the shadowlings and something monstrous bubbled within him. Was that rage? Alamakar considered himself a peaceful man, but he had no trouble showing his teeth when someone hurt his people.

The Old One would *pay*.

He drew more from the Essence, this time filling himself with her power. He would take it upon his own hands. Akin to the smokesmiths when breathing smoke, he was rejuvenated, as though he had ascended to divinity. Strength or weight didn't matter when he *was* power.

Alamakar waited for the devils to come. When they did, he propelled himself upwards. He greeted them with blows so powerful that traces of the Essence caused shockwaves as they were released. He grabbed one of the shad-owlings with both hands and ripped the creature in two. Heads detached from bodies, wings plucked out like wild-flowers, limbs torn off. He let out a fear-inducing roar of victory, but he found no glory in it. Only emptiness.

He shook himself when it was done.

*Doesn't feel any better, does it?*

This was war, and he had no time for feelings.

Alamakar flew yet again towards the royal chambers, dodging debris from the burning towers and fending off the creatures that sought to tear him to pieces. Still full of the Essence, he felt no danger, but ironically, it was *dangerous* not to. Carelessness got men killed.

Another shadowling flew towards him at great speed. Its mouth was agape, dozens of sharp fangs inside the powerful jaw. If a bite was probably enough to rip a man's head from his shoulders, Alamakar didn't want to find out what diseases it carried. He unsheathed *Red Perennial*, but just as he was about to fend off the demon, there was a pulse in his mind; a trickle of awareness—a sensation he had learned to attribute to the nearby presence of someone likewise attuned to the Essence.

He slashed the fiend anyway, cutting off its wings and causing it to crash down on a broken rooftop, then calmed himself so he could follow the thread to the source of the pulse. This level of probing was rarely attained by anyone other than the avatar, but even he couldn't tell exactly who it had been. All he knew was whoever it was, they were closing in on him, and fast.

Strengthening his grip on Red Perennial—one could never be too careful—he simply waited. The presence grew stronger by the second, and he breathed in relief as he saw a figure approach him.

"Red Sun! I'm glad you're well." Kasani's voice trembled as she stopped by him.

His worst fears hadn't come true then, as some of the battle sisters were still alive. "As am I. Where are your sisters?"

"Most of the battle sisters went on to the royal chambers to look for you there. They haven't come out yet. They are either still there or..."

Alamakar shook his head. "Don't say it. I'm on my way there now. How are the city's defensive efforts?"

"One of the squads managed to destroy a rift, but I imagine there are plenty more, my King. There have to be, with this many creatures..."

*The Deceiver's avatar can open them easily. We must hurry.*

"Stay out of the royal chambers, Kasani. Give aid to whoever needs it. Those are your orders."

Kasani took a second to respond. "What if it's a trap?"

Alamakar rested his hand on her pauldron. "I have to check on my family. And you know better than anyone that I will fight. I am ready, and so is the Essence."

Kasani nodded and stayed silent.

"Don't worry, Sister. The Deceiver will not win."

"I hear you, my King."

Alamakar conjured a smile of confidence but found himself more worried than confident. He turned to the royal chambers, thinking about the foulness that had installed itself there, at the very heart of the Essence. A parasite holding on for life. Zerike was there too, which worried him. Perhaps Agor could keep him safe. If only Alamakar had stayed there instead of going to the temple.

*Not going to the Temple, boy? Without meditation, how would you have cultivated my power into your body, then? No use thinking about that nonsense. Just go.*

Alamakar bit his lip. *Yes, Mother.*

Thunder boomed in the distance, and the sound of buildings collapsing was only deafened by the shrieks of panicked citizens as he made for the Palace of Brilliance first. The courtyard, large as it was, was infested by shadowlings of all shapes and sizes. Some spat fire and rocks, others flew like bats looking for prey.

He tapped into the Essence and shielded himself with her power and might.

*I need to focus.*

He took a deep breath and steadied himself. People thought of him as a flawless figure, a demigod of sorts, but he needed guidance and discipline just like everybody else.

*Be at ease. You have me.*

Those words almost soothed his soul.

Focusing on himself first and tapping into his Inner Flight, he followed the Essence's threads towards the Palace of Brilliance. These lines, invisible to most, manifested as a combination of pink and purple light that connected everything the Essence touched. He focused even harder, detaching himself from the threads that belonged to plants and lakes and rivers, focusing on the Palace of Brilliance.

Seeing real world locations through the Inner Flight was like grasping how they really were and all the energy embedded in them, sparse or organised in a complex web of energy flowing through every crevice of the city, as long as there was nature permeating it. All Alamakar had to do was follow these threads of the web with a gentle pull, like a weaver at the wheel, sorting out the threads and discarding those he didn't need. Every time he touched a thread of the Essence, he was flooded immediately with its purpose and gained immediate knowledge of which two points it connected.

He swallowed as he found some threads severely lacking the energy they needed, as though they'd been wounded—and he felt as though he'd been wounded by touching them.

*The Deceiver's corruption is already this deep...*

*All of it right under our noses,* the Essence replied.

Alamakar wondered if the Deceiver had been planning for this invasion for long. It had been decades since his last attempt, after all.

Alamakar was going to make him regret it.

*Oh, my poor boy*, the Essence said suddenly.

*What is it?*

The Essence remained silent at first. He searched for any irregularities, but besides the corruption, he had seen nothing noteworthy.

*Mother?* he insisted.

She was always so composed, which meant something had to be deeply wrong for her to react like that. Now she had gone quiet, which made it all the worse.

*Mother, what was it?*

She'd said "poor boy", but Alamakar was fine, which meant she was talking about someone else. Someone else he cared about.

"No..."

Alamakar cared about a lot of people, but only one warranted this kind of reaction.

*I'm so sorry, my boy.*

"Zerike..."

Alamakar abandoned the Inner Flight entirely and went back to feeling like a blind man again as his eyes opened. Activating the Essence's power, Alamakar ran inside the Palace of Brilliance, his heart racing. His mind spun, thinking of the possibilities, including the likeliest one of all: Zerike, his only heir, must have fallen to the Deceiver's minions.

As good as Alamakar was at handling pain, he had never felt as he did now, with his body moving on its own, fuelled by the hope that he was wrong. That hope was the sole driver of his rage. He tore through doors and walls and floors and ceilings. He tore creatures in half with a power he rarely liked to use, one that should be well-tamed. One that was good for nothing but causing pain. He felt monstrous, as though he had been corrupted.

His cool head was gone, replaced by a thirst for revenge and a calculated madness targeted at one thing only: the need to destroy the cause of his pain. The Deceiver.

Lost between the hope Zerike was alive and the devastating realisation that he might have died, Alamakar was trapped in an emotional vacuum. Too early to mourn. Too late to do something. All he could do was run late like he always did, hope for the best, and bear whatever pain he was supposed to endure.

Little by little, he shed off the mental and physical shackles that kept his powers subdued. As a king, he had to be wise and cold-headed, but if his intuition was right, this was not a time for kings but for desperate parents. With no cap on how much he could drink from the Essence, he was single-minded and focused on making sure Zerike was fine, refusing to relinquish hope. With every step he took, a looming sensation grew that he would only find more pain to bear. But with all limits to his power gone, there would be more pain for him to inflict.

And he was going to inflict plenty.

# EIGHT
# RUINS OF SMOKE

## ALAMAKAR

He must have passed hundreds of bodies on his way to the deeper chambers and twice as many fiendish creatures. They were like fleas. The Essence didn't need to talk to him when she trusted him to do the right thing. The mothering was over. Now Alamakar was going to fight on her behalf.

He burst through the door to Zerike's quarters, which were already half destroyed. Inside the chamber, he found a carnival of blood and gore, with his son standing still in the centre of it all. His eyes were lifeless and his skin pale. Alamakar went to him, but he could tell.

Zerike was dead.

No pulse. No breathing. Lifeless.

Even floating in the void that was the Essence's power, he felt his heart shatter. His joy was gone, his mind crushed by the pain. He was good at suffering, but nothing in the world could have prepared him for this.

He howled loudly at the pain and broke whatever windows weren't already broken. His spirit broke along with them. He hadn't even said goodbye, and now all he'd have would be memories of his boy tearing at his heart every day of his life, to remind him the real Zerike was gone. Alamakar screamed and shouted, hitting himself in the head, scratching himself in the face, blasting every breath of air in his lungs in mindless crying. When he finished, there was only emptiness.

He couldn't bear to look at Zerike's body. He tried, but he couldn't. It wasn't just the shock and the dark clutches death had on his heart; it was also the shame of being powerless. Shame of being too late. He was supposed to be king of the world, comparable to the sun, but in reality, he was no better than those who sold their children to the slave masters for half a coin.

In a fit of raging guilt, he took it all out on the rubble he'd caused, smashing his fists on rocks and throwing them in the air until he gave up, fell to his knees, and punched the ground lightly, his eyes welling up. As the tears built and fell, seasoning his grief, he realised the obvious: the world's most powerful man was weak. So weak he couldn't save his own son. So weak, he reacted like a thrashing child.

"Forgive me, Zerike. I—"

"Brother, I tried my best."

That voice gave Alamakar pause. He opened his eyes, wiped his tears, and looked at Agor.

He hadn't noticed his brother at first. There was something wrong with Agor. He smelled unnaturally rotten and foul. As soon as his eyes fell on him, he understood the betrayal, and it hurt even more. Agor had sided with the Deceiver.

"What did you say?"

Agor swallowed and looked away, allowing Alamakar to infer everything that had transpired before his arrival. He saw with clarity now, but that only made it worse. More pain for him to bear. His own brother, this time...

"How could you do this to me?" was all he could muster, his voice hollow.

He didn't just mean Zerike, of course. He meant the entire betrayal—siding with the Deceiver and becoming his avatar. His own brother!

Alamakar shouted in his mind, controlling the pain just enough to appear cool on the surface as he assessed his brother, who surely had enhanced abilities and powers gifted by the Deceiver.

Agor could barely look him in the eye. "I didn't mean to kill him. Well, I... I didn't actually kill him, it was just..."

Alamakar stayed silent and let him speak. Let Agor bear some of the pain, even if it would never make up for his loss.

"How could you?" Alamakar repeated. "What did he promise you that is worth more than your nephew's life?"

Agor grimaced and looked away again. There was no answer. He knew as well as Alamakar that nothing was worth the boy's life. Alamakar was going to make the Deceiver pay, and now that he had uncovered the truth, that meant making his brother pay. Zerike's death gave him the drive he needed and removed any pity or guilt he might have felt about getting rid of the Deceiver's new avatar.

Alamakar often wondered how he could make tainted people change their mind, but in this case, all he thought about was Zerike.

*Mother? The boy. Is there nothing to be done?*

*He was touched by the Old One, somehow.*

That was all the answer Alamakar needed.

He unleashed *Red Perennial* and charged Agor. The brother he knew was gone, corrupted; empowered by a force he thought he could comprehend.

*Ironic how this turned into a family affair. You against your brother and me against mine*, the Essence said.

But Alamakar barely listened.

The ancient, mighty sword clashed against Agor's dark blade. The weapon created another blast that tore down one of the pillars that held that wall of the chamber aloft. Alamakar pressed his brother as the wall crumbled into a cloud of dust. He didn't spare it a thought.

He just wanted Agor dead.

Alamakar cut and slashed and thrashed, striking Agor from overhead, left, and right, but at every blow, *Red Perennial* found his steel rival and sparks flew as the blades clanged and met again and again. But while Alamakar was on the balls of his feet and Agor on his heels, backing up at every blow, not letting any worry slip from his stony blank expression, never tripping in the rubble. Alamakar had duelled him too many times to ignore the fact that his brother was... holding back.

Alamakar managed to push him to the courtyard, now in an utter dismay of ruined buildings, destroyed cobbles, and burning wood frames. Agor took to the skies and Alamakar pursued with gritted teeth, *Red Perennial* ready to strike.

*Since when can he fly?*

Even as his blade moved to end Agor's life, when he looked at his brother, he saw the same shaggy hair loose in the wind as when they had ridden together to conquer the Nohani tribes. He saw the big blue eyes full of life as Alamakar picked him up from his crib for the first time. He saw the wooden sword fallen in the mud as a younger Agor cried, rubbing the big bump in his temple. Agor was still his baby brother; Alamakar wanted to hate him but couldn't.

Still, he didn't need hate to do what needed to be done. Hate was stifling and he needed to see like never before.

Most of the Palace of Brilliance had been destroyed and Ushar was in deep peril, but somehow the flying devils that had plagued the skies that evening must have been busy elsewhere. Of course, there was still loud roaring and shouting below. If death had a symphony, it would sound something like that.

Alamakar charged again. His celestial blade cut through the sky, creating a blast of power that extended from horizon to horizon. Agor defended the strike with his blade, straining to control the shock of the blow. Alamakar didn't give him any rest. He struck from overhead, then switched stances and struck from the right.

*Red Perennial* would not break, he knew that, but blows like those could not be stopped by normal blades, which meant the one Agor held had to be a gift from his new lord.

"I was going to try and convince you to join me, but it's too late, isn't it?" Agor asked. "Too late for you to abandon this drunken state of madness she puts you in."

The nerve.

Alamakar charged again without a response. How dare he speak when he was the corrupted one? "You killed your own nephew. My son."

Agor nodded as he strained to resist Alamakar's blade. "And that's something I will have to live with for the rest of my life."

Alamakar gritted his teeth. "Don't worry. You won't live much longer."

His brother shook his head and parried *Red Perennial* away. "Don't you see it? She treats you like a pawn and controls your every move."

"Die, brother." Alamakar spat the last word. He had to complete his purpose as the Essence's avatar and destroy the Deceiver. That meant wiping Agor off the face of the world, and he had no issues with that.

The weight of Alamakar's blows became heavier, each movement embedded with power from the Essence. *Red Perennial* was a vehicle for his power, every strike causing gusts of wind around it at first, but Agor parried the blows, matching Alamakar's intensity. Every cut his brother dodged or parried sent a blast of energy down towards the courtyard, obliterating the surrounding chaos.

Alamakar pushed forward, but so did Agor, their blades locked in a contest of strength that created ripples of heat and light in the air around them. Since Agor could match him in power, Alamakar tried speed, too. His strikes became faster and harder to predict, and so the blades clashed again and again as Alamakar and Agor moved in the sky, looming above everyone and everything.

I need more power. More speed.

*If I remember correctly, you took the liberty of removing the limitations you had in place,* the Essence said.

Alamakar roared and charged Agor again with a blast. He didn't need his blade to touch Agor any longer. In the trance of the battle with his brother, Alamakar didn't know if they were still above Ushar or if they'd moved somewhere else. He knew that wherever they went, they'd bring destruction with them. But he couldn't back down now. He needed to end Agor once and for all.

Agor's face spelled out similar thoughts. "I hate having to kill you, brother, but the Essence must be destroyed."

"It is you"—Alamakar gritted his teeth as he pushed his blade forwards to bite into Agor—"who must die."

Alamakar became more powerful as time went on. His strikes opened craters on the ground, but so did Agor's. If he took his eyes from his brother, he would probably get cut badly.

Then he dove into his Inner Flight. In his state, he could do so without losing his physical awareness, not even for a second. Up there, with only Agor to contend with and no distractions, he was more in tune with himself.

His blade cut through Agor's shoulder, and he hissed but then smirked as the wound healed. "You always claimed first blood. But tell me, who ended up winning? Be honest."

"We're not children any longer, Agor. At least I am not."

Those words tore into his brother more than the sword did, judging by the way he frowned and snarled. Every time the blades clashed, their power reverberated through

Alamakar's arms, then his body, to be released into the world, caring not what lay beneath.

Agor took a step back and hurried away from the exchange. Alamakar initially thought he had overwhelmed his brother, but soon realised Agor was just trying to find space for a move. As he retreated, Agor reached for something in the air, mimicking a pulling motion and opening a rift, blue sparks buzzing.

*Careful, boy. He's not playing any longer.*

Alamakar nodded. "It seems like old dogs *do* learn new tricks."

Agor bit his lip. He pulled something invisible in the sky and as he did, Alamakar almost lost control of his body, as though gravity no longer applied to him. As though he could no longer fly. Agor moved his arm to the right, and an invisible force pulled Alamakar to the right as well, in a motion similar to Agor's arm movement.

*How do I stop him?*

*Go and finish him.*

That was all he needed to hear. He stopped resisting whatever magnetic force was pulling him, and fell on top of his brother.

They wrestled like children, sneaking punches and chokes at each other while they grappled for control of each other's hands and weapons. Then Agor smiled, and Alamakar realised they were no longer in the sky but somewhere completely different.

"Welcome to the aether, brother," Agor said.

"What is this place?"

Agor must have used that pulling force to drag Alamakar to whatever this place was. It was like a completely dark sky but with no ground underneath. The only available light was the purple hue of faraway stars. They were in an endless pool of nothingness.

"It's everything. The past. The present. The future. The Old One's realm."

Suddenly, Alamakar felt something about him changing. A weariness creeping onto his shoulders.

*What is he doing to me?*

*Not him, the Deceiver. He's meddling with time to make you old and frail.*

Alamakar scoffed. He was already old, but never frail. Under the Essence's blessing, he would remain unaffected by the ages, no matter how fast they came and went.

A look of frustration settled on Agor's face. "Interesting."

Alamakar wasn't as uncomfortable in the void as perhaps Agor had assumed he would be. He didn't have the Deceiver's Temporal Exploration, but he was well familiar with it and with how he had used rifts to travel through ages come and past. How he could wind the passing of time like a stringed spinning top toy.

But the Deceiver wasn't that great in combat. That's why he needed to deceive his followers. Perhaps that's why he had picked Agor as his new avatar—his brother had been a general, trained in combat for decades, if not centuries. There was no weapon he couldn't wield.

"My turn." Alamakar tensed and a surge of power ran through his veins, carrying nearly more of the Essence than he could hold. His vision blurred, but he didn't need to see with the Inner flight. His body heated, but he didn't need it when the Essence gave him strength to ascend to realms beyond mortality. His moment had come; he was ready.

There, in the vacuum, Alamakar exploded.

Bits of burnt flesh and bone moved through the nothingness, along with blood. All torn to pieces, now floating in the aether. It hurt almost as much as losing Zerike, almost as much as all the guilt and shame that came with knowing he had a treacherous brother.

*But I've always been good at bearing pain.*

Agor's wide eyes betrayed a hint of wonder and fear—he hadn't seen this coming. The Deceiver couldn't have predicted it. Agor looked dumbfounded as Alamakar watched him from his light spiritual body, a remnant of his former self which had emerged from his flesh and bones, but more alive now than ever. Abandoning his ties to the mortal realm had been his fate as the Essence's avatar, and he had long known this day would come.

Agor still looked left and right, looking for Alamakar, perhaps expecting him to strike him from behind, perhaps expecting this to be a wild miscalculation on his part. Part of Alamakar enjoyed watching him powerless. This was supposed to be his realm, wasn't it? The Deceiver's realm.

He tried to speak to his brother, to tell him this was no trick, no charade, but Agor couldn't see him at all, so Alamakar couldn't speak to him, either.

*What now?* he asked the Essence. *How do we win?*

*Now you become what you were always meant to be.*

Ever since he was a boy chosen to be the avatar, he knew he was destined to ascend to the heavens, to shed off his mortal skin and become a powerful spirit with the soul of a dragon. He'd fight the Deceiver on the Essence's behalf. The world's fate rested on the result of that fight. For decades, he doubted the veracity of those promises, but here he was, halfway through his ascension, which would undoubtedly involve smoke.

He was no longer a mortal, but he was impatient still. What if Agor decided to open a rift and he was stuck there?

The urgency in his thoughts seemed to have sped up his transformation. It didn't take long for smoke to appear from the bits of his torn corpse. In the vacuum, the smoke clung to the organic matter first.

"What is this?" Agor asked. "Old One? What is happening?"

If the Old One spoke to Agor, it was directly to his mind.

Alamakar knew what to do. He had spent years meditating, shaping his spirit and strengthening his soul for this very moment. Just as he'd practiced a million times in his Inner Flight, he curdled the smoke tightly, as though crafting a rope. He channelled his own fresh understanding of the Essence and kept the smoke growing. Agor tried to dissipate the smoke, but it was futile.

After the smoke didn't dissipate, Agor cursed himself and unsheathed his dark blade—perhaps expecting something nefarious. Meanwhile, Alamakar worked to weave himself into the threads of smoke that were coming together.

*So far so good, boy. He can't ensnare me if I don't hold a body. But we must be careful. He can still end us.*

*Yes, Mother.*

Alamakar kept going, curdling the smoke and thickening it to form an enormous chain-like undulation, becoming a part of it.

"This smoke. How do I make it stop?" Agor asked, though the Deceiver must not have responded.

*Can you sense him, Mother? The Deceiver?*

*Always, my boy. Every waking moment. For all eternity.*

The threads of smoke tightened and thickened fast, flowing in the aether with purpose and with Alamakar's spirit now thoroughly woven into them. It didn't take long for him to grow a face in the smoke, just not his own. The magic smoke became denser, and the facial features became sharper by the second. Horns first, then a long snout with a hundred sharp teeth in the mouth.

With the smoke a physical manifestation of the Essence's power, just as he was, he was slowly becoming a dragon of smoke, the undulating threads turning into a long, serpentine body.

He *had become* the embodiment of smoke.

Roaring, Alamakar willed two massive smoke wings on his back, and they spread, spanning the height of five men from end to end.

Alamakar relished the horror on Agor's face as his brother watched him blossom into a full-sized dragon of smoke. He could almost read the panic in his face. With no physical body, Alamakar would be hard—if not impossible—to kill. Even if he managed to dissipate the shape of the smoke dragon, Alamakar could simply reshape the threads again.

Desperate, Agor moved to strike with his blade again, but Alamakar had seen it in his Inner Flight and grabbed hold of him with the dragon's mouth before he could do such a thing. Agor looked shocked upon realising the dragon had moved so much faster than he could, and even more so that the smoke dragon was as solid as a smoke weapon could be. Alamakar couldn't have asked for a better gift from the Essence than this.

*Your little stunt is over, Brother.*

Agor struggled to free himself.

It was useless to resist. Alamakar moved faster than lightning, back towards the rift Agor had opened. He dragged his brother through it along with him; there was a certain pressure before they found themselves once again in the Known World. Alamakar still hadn't finished his job. Agor was still alive and the Deceiver was still capable of destroying the Essence, even now he was no longer in his realm.

Agor freed himself from the dragon's mouth, but Alamakar charged at him, completely covered in the Essence, his long body flowing in the sky like a snake swimming in water. She had provided solutions when all he had were problems and pain. The world had thrived and prospered because of her. As her avatar, Alamakar had to keep her alive at all costs.

Suddenly, Agor contorted and looked as though he was going to vomit. He retched and retched, until a viscous white tentacle shot out from his throat. Two more slithered their way out of his mouth and Agor cried in pain.

*He's here, boy,* the Essence said. *He's here.*

Alamakar understood.

The foulness he'd been smelling was now incarnate as the Deceiver pulled himself out of Agor. Faster and faster, the tentacles ripped their way out of Agor's body. More tentacles burst from his crotch, his armpits, and his waist. The Deceiver wore Agor like a ragged sock puppet. Alamakar counted four tentacles on each side, two looming above the head and another four along Agor's lifeless legs.

*He's still finding his footing, boy. What are you waiting for? Envelop him. This is our chance!*

Alamakar listened to the Essence and, with his long, draconic body, wrapped himself around the Deceiver, pushing against the slippery tentacles. He shifted the shape of the smoke into a ball-like prison to contain the Deceiver. Exerting that much pressure to keep that form intact hurt Alamakar, even with the Essence's power behind him. This time, he wasn't facing a human he could push around like a rag doll, but an otherworldly entity.

Pain. So much pain.

The Deceiver worked to escape Alamakar's enveloping prison, shooting and pinching Alamakar's mind. The Deceiver's foulness was upon him, but Alamakar resisted the pain and the hurt. This was what Alamakar had been born to do, and he was going to do it. For Zerike, Ushar, and the world.

For the Essence, he would bear pain.

Embracing the struggle, he squeezed the Deceiver.

Images flashed through his mind. He wasn't sure if that was the work of the Deceiver or if he was reaching the end of his life. First, he saw himself and Agor wrestling against the waves, always with a smile on their faces as they dreamt of fighting forces much stronger than them. Then he saw Zerike born, a beautiful and strong baby boy, crying his heart out straight from his mother's womb. In that moment, Alamakar had known Zerike was destined for greatness.

How wrong he had been.

And Zerike's mother, Zerifia, crying in pain, sweating, covered in blood. Her chest heaving, her eyes closing. Alamakar had never seen someone so strong in his life as he held her hand, gripping it tightly even as she lost consciousness and her eyes closed, never to open again. Then he saw himself alone in the sky, a ball of sturdy smoke trapping a god.

*So much for my immortality.*

Still, this was duty. And the only thing he had to fight for.

*That's it! Squeeze, Alamakar! Contain him, my boy!*

Alamakar saw glimpses of the Essence's past. All the pain and torture the Deceiver had inflicted on her in ages long gone. Those were her memories seeping into his mind, or perhaps a carnival or delirium architected by his own brain to make his pain seem minor.

He enveloped the Deceiver in smoke until they shrank to the size of a child's toy.

*Alamakar*, the Essence called. *You've done well. Now it's my turn. I'm fading out, but so is he. The world will have peace again. You shall remain with me. Just know I'm proud of you.*

*I'm proud of you.*

*I'm proud of you.*

*I'm proud of you.*

Those words rang in Alamakar's mind. The only words he had ever wanted to hear.

# Epilogue

The Essence embedded herself in the ball of smoke that enveloped the Old One. Alamakar had done well.

Using every bit of her strength, she shrank further and turned the smoke into a crystal. It was so small... the size of a pendant for a necklace.

*Bury this orb and let no one find it,* she spoke into the minds of her followers.

They'd find this red orb after she perished and they'd hide it. With the Old One trapped, there would finally be peace, even if she would be gone too.

No... those were Alamakar's naïve words of hope. Not hers.

Peace was only temporary.

THE END

# Also by the Author

Ruins of Smoke (Prequel novella)
Seeds of War (The Smokesmiths Book 1)

# Thank you! Please Read!

You've made it!

I cannot thank you enough for choosing to spend your precious time in my company. Or rather, accompanied by the characters in *Ruins of Smoke*. Without readers, I would write stories for myself. And where's the fun in that? I've been lucky enough that the initial reception for *Seeds of War* has been fantastic, so *Ruins of Smoke* is my token of gratitude to every single person who has championed my work.

If you enjoyed *Ruins of Smoke* and haven't picked up *Seeds of War* yet, consider doing so, since you have a pretty good idea by now of what to expect from this series. Please consider leaving a review on Amazon and on Goodreads. In the avalanche of books being published every single day, we indie authors need absolutely every bit of help we can get. I can promise you there is no better help than leaving a review for a book.

While writing *Seeds of War* had all the bumps in the road normal in a debut novel, *Ruins of Smoke* had its challenges too. Writing four points of view in such a short novella without losing the emotional core of the book was a challenge, to say the least. Ultimately, this was a story of bonds, connections and family. It's a story of people learning to fight for their loved ones, those going against the grain to achieve meaningful change, and those who need to fight their demons and misconceptions to find their true strength. It's also a story of strength and weakness, and how thin the line can be between the two.

I will keep writing, so you keep reading!

Stay strong, always.
João F. Silva

# JOIN THE
# SMOKESMITHS

Sign up to João F. Silva's mailing list at www.joaofsilva
.net to get the digital version of *Ruins of Smoke* and his
short story *A Dead Man,* both for FREE. You'll be the
first to receive all the news, writing updates regarding *The
Smokesmiths* series, any other projects or special offers and
discounts.

# Acknowledgments

This book is for everyone who has supported my writing journey so far.

In the three months that followed the publication of *Seeds of War*, it was hard to put any words to paper. There was anxiety and excitement. There was fear that the book would tank. Luckily, I struck gold by finding an amazing online community of readers, bloggers, reviewers and other authors who have read, reviewed and championed my writing since its inception. I cannot stress enough how helpful it was to have this level of support and positivity around me while writing this novella.

I have to thank my editor Sarah Chorn first. She is a wizard with words who turns average manuscripts into pretty good ones. Her keen eye and experience helped me kick this novella into reading shape. Writing powerful emotions is hard, and I doubt anyone can identify them and write them as well as she can. Without her helping hand, a lot of key moments in this book would have surely fallen flat.

My proofreader Ed Crocker, who is a lifesaver and an extremely talented writer, was the last line of defence in the war against typos and pesky mistakes. Thanks to his work, *Ruins of Smoke* evolved into its final form.

Many other beta readers provided extremely insightful feedback, of course! They are legends who don't mind reading a second or third draft just to help me polish it. What more could I ask for? So many people in the indie reading and writing community have supported me from day one. Sean Halpin, Nick Procter, and Charlie Cavendish read *Seeds of War* in the very early days and have been my absolute champions over these past three months. I wish every author could have people as amazing as them to support them in their endeavours.

As always, I also have to thank my wife, who never rolled her eyes or made fun of my love for fantasy and writing. Instead, she has given me nothing but love, support and understanding ever since I told her: "I think I want to write books."

And that's what I'll keep doing!

# About the Author

João F. Silva was born in a small town in Portugal but now lives in London, with his three feline co-workers/bosses. He writes Epic Fantasy, Science Fiction and Horror and has been on the jury for the 2020 and 2022 editions of the "Best Newcomer" Award at the British Fantasy Awards. His short fiction was published in Grimdark Magazine and Haven Speculative.

Get in touch by filling in the form on his website (www .joaofsilva.net), by emailing him at joao@joaofsilva.net or by following him on social media.

# GLOSSARY

Belleaf Oil – Highly flammable oil extracted from belleaf flowers. Doesn't require a spark to start burning. Often used by smokesmiths.

Inner Flight – A method of harnessing the Essence's blessing for enhanced personal and spatial awareness.

Lantern Horn – Humanoid fish-like creature with a horn growing from its forehead that lights up on occasion.

Spitfire – Giant reptilian demon with a bulky body, which spits fire and molten rocks.

Red Perennial – Ancient red sword owned and wielded by Alamakar, the Red Sun King.

Shadesgrowl – Large yet slow herbivore creature used as a mount in cold climates.

Smokesmith – Person who is able to breathe smoke and has the ability to manipulate it.

Smoke Riders – A title given to the smokesmiths who are able to take flight and ride smoke clouds as well as summon weapons of smoke.

Timeless – Agor's dark-coloured sword gifted to him by the Old One.

Ushar – Capital of the Usharian Empire. The largest city in the Known World.

Usharian Empire – Governing force which expands throughout the entire Known World, ruled by the Red Sun King, Alamakar.

Zeiram Bastion – Headquarters of the eastern division of the Sentinels. Home base of Jeha and many other battle sisters.

# Dramatis Personae

Jeha – Battle sister and sentinel of the Red Sun Army.

The Essence – Deity or entity that controls nature, and lends her powers and smoke magic to specific people in the Usharian Empire.

Amel – Legendary battle sister and sentinel of the Red Sun Army.

Rosach – Battle sister and sentinel of the Red Sun Army.

Olon – Battle sister and sentinel of the Red Sun Army.

Shakil – Battle sister and sentinel of the Red Sun Army.

The Deceiver (or The Old One) – Deity or entity that manipulates time, and lends his power to a chosen avatar.

Agor – General of the Red Sun Army. Brother of Alamakar, Uncle of Zerike. Avatar of the Old One.

Sohara – Battle sister and sentinel of the Red Sun Army.

Zerike – Young prince and heir to the Usharian Empire. Son of Alamakar, nephew of Agor.

Matala – Smokesmith, Smoke Rider apprentice and youngest member of the Douser unit of the Red Sun Army.

Dugala – Matala's master. Smoke Rider and also part of the Dousers.

Telafa – Master Smoke rider and also part of the Dousers.

Alamakar – The Red Sun King, ruler of the Known World and supreme leader of the Usharian Empire. Avatar of the Essence. Zerike's father.

Poonama – Battle sister and sentinel of the Red Sun Army.

Kasani – Battle sister and sentinel of the Red Sun Army.